'Tess...you
murmured.

Tessa broke away from his kisses and pulled back, breathing hard. 'We should make tracks. My grandmother will be wondering where we've got to.'

Luke was watching her, his gaze narrowed and assessing. 'And where have we got to, Tess?' he asked quietly.

She drew in a shallow breath. Was he issuing a deliberate challenge? At the possibility, she felt her nerve-ends shred. She couldn't think about the rest of the day, or even tomorrow—let alone the future.

What future? He was going away...

Leah Martyn comes from a long line of storytellers. As well as her Medical Romances™, she has written and published short stories. Her home is with her husband in rural Queensland, Australia. She describes her garden as her special delight, its abundance of Australian native plants attracting birdlife in large numbers. Living in an area rich in heritage, she finds walking heritage trails a fascinating pastime.

Recent titles by the same author:

THE DOCTORS' MARRIAGE
THE VISITING CONSULTANT

THE ER AFFAIR

BY
LEAH MARTYN

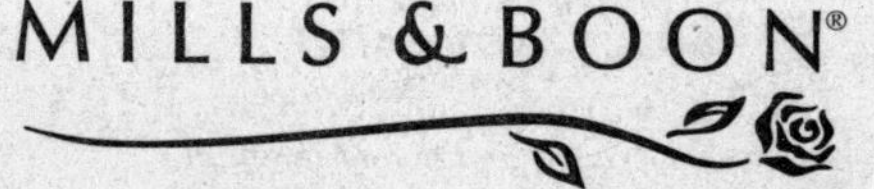

First published in Great Britain 2002
Harlequin Mills & Boon Limited,
Eton House, 18-24 Paradise Road, Richmond, Surrey TW9 1SR

ISBN 0 263 83084 5

Set in Times Roman 10½ on 12¼ pt.
03-0802-41717

Printed and bound in Spain
by Litografia Rosés, S.A., Barcelona

CHAPTER ONE

TESSA willed a quiet end to the last hour of her late shift. On a Saturday night in A and E? Was she being an optimist or what?

Putting the treatment room to rights yet again, she deplored their lack of trained staff. For whatever reasons, regional and rural hospitals seemed to be the last places anyone with decent credentials wanted to work.

Thankfully, the Health Department had begun a new initiative, encouraging city-based senior doctors to be generous with their time and skills and contract to do locums in rural hospitals.

But could they really hope to attract an SR here to Cressbrook? Already, they'd had two non-starters. But on the other hand, why not? As Queensland country towns went, it had everything going for it.

Of course, she was just the tiniest bit biased. Tessa's mouth curved wryly. But when you were born and raised in the bush, perhaps you were linked for ever. Just the scent of wood smoke and the dry crackle of wind through the gum trees was enough to turn her insides to mush.

With deft precision, she quickly sorted and tidied the sterile supplies, guessing the old saying was true—you could take the girl out of the country but you could never take the country out of the girl…

'There's a drugs overdose and an MVA sole occupant coming in.' Charge Sue Mitchell popped her head around the door. 'Which do you want?'

'You mean I have a choice?' Tessa laughed drily as she reached for an apron. 'If it's all the same to you, I'll take the motor vehicle.'

'Want a bit of good news?' Sue raised a dark brow. 'We've secured the services of a senior registrar for the next three months.'

Tessa looked sceptical. 'Signed and sealed?'

'Starting on Monday.'

'Hallelujah! Male or female, do we know?'

'Oh, definitely male.' Sue swooped on a pile of clean linen. 'Luke Stretton.'

Tessa frowned. Something about the name rang a bell. She shrugged, dismissing the thought. It was probably nothing. The sirens caterwauling in the distance brought her back to reality with a snap. 'Up and at 'em again, then.' The two young women exchanged a commiserating look and hurried towards the ambulance bay.

'Want me to take the report?' Their shift was almost over and Tessa had noticed that Sue had become a bit restive, glancing surreptitiously at her watch.

'Would you mind?' Sue made an apologetic small face. 'We're still trying to function with only one car and Iain would've finished at the golf club ten minutes ago. By the time I get out there to pick him up—'

'Go.'

'Are you sure?'

Tessa made a shooing motion with her hands. 'I can be home in a few minutes.'

'Thanks, Tess. I owe you one. It's still bucketing down out there.' Sue burrowed into a raincoat and turned up the collar.

'It's only a storm,' Tessa dismissed airily. 'And think of the fabulously clear morning we'll have tomorrow.'

'Think of the lawn another foot higher, you mean.'

Tessa chuckled. 'Drive carefully.'

'These days I've every good reason to.' Sue smiled mistily, her hand going instinctively to her tummy. 'See you when I see you, then.'

Thoughtfully, Tessa went along to the staffroom to make herself a hot drink. Sue and her husband were over the moon, and rightly so. After five years of marriage, Sue had finally managed to conceive.

At the window Tessa sipped her tea, reflecting she'd never really met a man she'd wanted to have a child with. Not if you discounted Will Carter. With his Geordie accent and rough-hewn, off-beat handsomeness, he'd attracted her like a moth to a flame.

She'd thought they had something wonderful together, fully expected him to renew his contract with St Anne's Hospital in Brisbane where they'd both worked. But after his three months had expired, he'd told her he hadn't been quite truthful about his marital status. He was separated but now he looked like patching things up with his wife. He was going home.

Tessa shook her head, as if to clear it. Why on earth was she even giving Will Carter headroom? He'd proved himself an opportunistic rat. Don't look back, she counselled herself silently. It was unproductive and pointless.

But very difficult to carry out.

Moving closer to the window-pane, she peered out at the bright quivers of lightning. With her country upbringing, she was familiar with the pattern of south-east Queensland summer storms and how they could strike with dangerous ferocity and peter out just as quickly.

She just hoped they wouldn't lose power. Although the hospital generators would kick in almost immediately, there'd be no such joy at home and there was something decidedly eerie about fumbling your way around in the pitch darkness.

'It's foul out there!' Drew McIntosh, the charge for the night shift, squelched his way in. 'Any tea going?'

'Help yourself. Water's just boiled.'

Drew joined her at the window, nursing his steaming mug and a handful of rich tea biscuits. 'Energy hit.' He sent her a wry smile. 'Been busy?'

Tessa sent her gaze briefly to the ceiling. 'Not so you'd notice.'

Drew's brow furrowed. 'This rain is bound to trigger a few pile-ups. Who's the MO on duty?'

'Brad Metcalf,' Tessa said, referring to their resident.

Drew groaned.

'He's young and a bit over-zealous.' Tessa was kind. 'Cut him a bit of slack.'

'Who's around for backup?'

'Heaven knows.' Tessa blocked a yawn. 'The good news is that a locum reg. is supposedly arriving next week.'

The rest of the night shift began to straggle in.

'Things are crazy out there. Looks like we'll be in for a wild old night,' one of the junior RNs predicted with ghoulish anticipation.

'Would anyone mind if we get on with handover?' Tessa raised her voice above the din. 'I'd really like to get home this side of midnight.'

Suddenly, the lights flickered and were gone. A general moan went up, followed automatically by a cheer as the emergency power sprang into life.

Tessa completed the report with economical swiftness. Nevertheless, she was the last to leave the building after the shift. The car park was in darkness, the rain lashing down, a mean, howling wind joining in, whipping her dark hair around her face.

With her borrowed umbrella, she ran for her four-wheel-drive Jeep, guided only by the light from the pencil torch she always carried. So far, so good, she congratulated herself, unlocking the driver's door and flinging herself inside. She lifted a hand, scooping damp tendrils away from her collar. She felt grubby and tired, and she longed for home, a shower and bed.

The streetlights were unlit. Tessa tamped down her unease, switching to high beam as she slid into the tree-lined street beyond the car park.

Had they replaced the candles at home? she fretted. It was anyone's guess how long the power would be down. Please, let it be on again by the morning. Having to go without her wake-up mug of coffee was unthinkable…

'What the—?' Her rambling conjectures were interrupted by the sudden appearance of an obviously male figure on the road in front of her. And as if that wasn't enough, he was waving her down.

Tessa swallowed. 'I don't need this,' she muttered. Whatever the circumstances, stopping for persons unknown was asking for trouble, but in the middle of the night…an absolute no-no.

On the other hand, perhaps this person did have a genuine emergency. After all, they were very close to the hospital…

In a second her caring instincts overcame her unease. She braked, almost instinctively putting the vehicle into reverse gear. If he *was* trouble, she'd have the Jeep back into the hospital precincts like a speeding bullet. Activating the interior light, she waited.

Within seconds of her stopping, the man loomed large and dark at her driver's window, bending almost double to peer inside. Tessa wound the window down a fraction, her courage subsiding into goosebumps and a wildly beating heart. 'What do you want?' She heard her voice husky and uneven. 'I've got my mobile—so no funny business, OK?'

'Funny business is the last thing on my mind,' the man growled. 'I'm whacked and fed-up, trying to find the doctors' residence in this God-forsaken place. I've been round the block three times and there's nothing to tell me where I've been or where I should be going to.' His gaze homed in on her nurse's uniform. 'But I see my luck's about to change. You obviously work at the hospital?'

'Tessa O'Malley.' She lowered the window halfway. 'And you are?'

'Luke Stretton.'

'You're the new SR?' Tessa's eyes widened in disbelief. 'Why on earth are you travelling at this time of night?'

'It's a long story.' He sounded irritable. 'I just want a shower and a bed.'

Tessa pulled back from his sudden closeness, almost tasting the mingled scents of his aftershave and the sweet sharpness of the rain. Taking a controlling breath, she glared at him over the pane of glass separating them. 'The doctors' quarters are not attached to the actual hospital but kind of at the back, an old colonial home. But it has access through the grounds to the hospital.'

'On a fine day, I'd probably find all this information riveting.' Luke Stretton flicked his damp hair impatiently, so that it flopped towards his eyes. 'But for the present, Sister O'Malley, if you'd cut to the chase and just point me in the general direction, I'd be eternally grateful.'

Disagreeable man! If he didn't want to work in a rural environment, why on earth had he agreed to come to Cressbrook in the first place? Tessa felt like taking off and leaving him standing there. Instead, she relented, grabbing her umbrella and swinging out of the Jeep. Snapping the hood up over their heads, she asked pointedly, 'Where are you parked?'

'Just here, in someone's driveway.' He made a backward thumbing motion towards a dark, low-slung vehicle. 'I was about to forget the whole thing and find a motel when I saw your lights.'

And spooked the life out of her.

'Right. You'll need to go halfway back along this street, turn left and then— Look...' She waved a dismissive hand. 'It's probably easier all round if I lead and you follow. You'll never find it in the rain. And all the streetlights are out.'

'I had noticed.'

Tessa gave an impatient twitch of her shoulder. 'If you're ready, then?'

'Thanks,' he responded gruffly, and looked straight into her eyes. 'I'll reverse out and follow you.'

Looking at him in the dim light, his hair, sleekly black from the rain, his long legs encased in faded denim and the collar of his battered leather jacket turned up against the storm, Tessa felt the sudden unsteadiness to her breathing.

Even allowing for the fact he was soaked, dishevelled and obviously cross, Cressbrook's new senior registrar exuded sex appeal in spades.

Home at last, Tessa pulled into the dual carport. The sensor light came on as she walked up the stairs and onto the porch. She gave a silent cheer. With the power back on, she could indulge in a hot shower before she fell into bed.

Opening the front door, she tiptoed inside. All was quiet. Tessa gave a wry smile. Her friend and housemate, Alison James, was on earlies and probably fast asleep, oblivious of the wild storm they'd just had.

Tessa went through to her bedroom, relieved all over again that the practicality of sharing her house was working out so well, mostly because she and Alison were aware of the stress of their jobs and mindful of each other's needs as a result.

Dumping her bag on the window seat, she stopped for a moment in front of the mirror. She looked like hell, she decided ruefully, releasing the heavy mass of dark curls from their restraining butterfly clip to tumble around her shoulders.

Peering closer, she brushed the tips of her fingers across her cheekbones. Her complexion wasn't doing her any favours either. Her skin looked pasty and washed out and her eyes resembled a badly made-up panda's.

She shrugged. No wonder Dr Stretton had looked at her a bit oddly. Well, who cared anyway? Shift-work took its toll on the body. Thank heavens she had tomorrow off. Then it was back to earlies on Monday. But that wasn't so bad, not when she had the prospect of a three-day break to look forward to at the end of the week.

Luke looked around his bedroom. It was better than he'd expected, large, airy and with plenty of wardrobe space. Not that he'd brought much with him.

He expected his three-month contract with the hospital to consist of nothing but work. But at the end of it he'd be free and clear of his obligation to the Health Department.

A flicker of irritation crossed his face. He couldn't believe the conditions they'd slapped on him, using some kind of departmental-speak, terming it, 'mutual obligation'. In other words, if he accepted a government-funded package to pursue advanced surgical training overseas, he had to be prepared to put something back into the public health system here. And in this case, it was rural public health where the need was paramount.

He gave a small grimace. It was odd the way life

panned out sometimes. Just when he'd thought he'd had his future all mapped out, fate had sent him a curved ball.

Unzipping his case, he grabbed a pair of sleep shorts and a towel and headed off to find the bathroom.

In the shower, he lathered himself, letting the warm jet of water spray over his head and slick down over his chest and shoulders to puddle around his feet. For better or worse, he was here in Cressbrook and, despite his reasons for coming here, he intended to give it his best shot. But at the end of his contract he didn't expect to be any more attracted to a rural lifestyle than he'd ever been.

Turning off the shower, he slicked back his hair. He'd cope. Hell! He was a multi-skilled professional. And if he was needed in Theatre occasionally, it could only help to relieve the boredom of working in the bush.

Sleep wouldn't come.

For the umpteenth time, Luke switched positions, punching up the pillows behind him. He was wound up. It had been a very full day. Perhaps, after all, it hadn't been the brightest idea to have hit the road straight after his brother's wedding. But he'd had nothing stronger than a couple of light beers throughout the evening and he'd been packed anyway…

But then he'd had to run into the damn storm. *And* Sister Tessa O'Malley. His chest rose in a chuckle. He'd have had to have been unconscious not to remember *her*!

Gorgeous? She was that all right. A grin stretched

his lips and his body began to relax. Perhaps his stint in rural medicine would have its compensations after all. Especially if Tessa O'Malley was around.

Tessa woke late. An unwilling glance at the bedside clock told her it was already midmorning. Hunching up a shoulder, she snuggled down under the covers once more, hovering blissfully in the gentle twilight between wakefulness and sleep.

Nevertheless, by the time Alison had arrived home from her shift at three-thirty, Tessa had managed to tidy the house and herself and had a pot of freshly brewed coffee waiting.

'Mmm, that smells divine.' Throwing her shoulder-bag over a nearby peg rail, Alison dropped into a chair. 'My feet are killing me!'

Tessa chuckled. 'Same old, same old. Here, get this into you.' Pouring a mug of fragrant coffee, she passed it across. 'And I made something for afternoon tea.' With a flourish, she whipped away a tea-towel, revealing a still-warm banana cake.

'Oh, yum!' Alison helped herself to a large slice. 'Mmm…' she managed around a mouthful. 'The rumour mill was running at top speed today. Guess what I heard?'

'That we're getting a new SR in A and E,' Tessa said blandly. 'Luke Stretton.'

'You knew!' Alison wailed her disappointment. 'When's he due in town?'

Tessa lifted a shoulder. 'He's here already. I ran into him last night outside the hospital in all that rain.'

'What?' Alison snickered. 'Actually ran into him?'

Tessa rolled her eyes. 'I know I've sideswiped the odd lamppost but, no, I didn't actually *run* into him. Dr Stretton wanted directions for the doctors' residence. He flagged me down.'

'So—' Alison's dark eyes gleamed '—how did he seem? A plus for our talent pool?'

Tessa snorted inelegantly. 'If you like hedgehogs!'

'Bit prickly, was he?'

'He called Cressbrook a "God-forsaken place", for heaven's sake!'

Alison sent her friend a dry look. 'I can see you hit it off. Listen, Tess, not everyone is as passionate about the bush as you are.' She licked a scattering of sticky crumbs from her fingers. 'But, hey! Wouldn't it be a hoot if he turned out to be your Mr Right?'

'As if!' Tessa's heart fluttered in alarm. 'What makes you think I'm looking for Mr Right, anyway?'

'At our age, kiddo,' Alison sighed dramatically, 'aren't we all?'

Jerking up from her chair, Tessa poured the rest of her coffee down the sink. 'Speaking for myself, I've more to do with my time than take up with locum doctors! Especially big-city types!'

'Aren't you protesting a little too much, Tessa?' Alison teased good-naturedly. Propping her chin on her hand, she said thoughtfully, 'I must take a wander through A and E next shift and check out your Luke Stretton.'

Tessa's heart was all but leapfrogging against her chest wall as she slipped into the hospital for the start of her early shift on Monday.

She was being ridiculous, she berated herself. Personality-wise, she'd worked with some of the best and worst registrars in her time. If Luke Stretton fell somewhere in between, they'd probably rub along. And he was here for three months only. If things got tough, she'd have to remember that.

Going into the office, she took the report from Drew who was finishing his rota of night duty. Tessa could see they'd been busy. 'The child with the query appendix?' She noted the nine-year-old had been brought in at five-thirty.

'He's back from Theatre and on the ward. It was a rush job. He was on the point of rupture when they opened him up. Our reg. made himself available for the op.'

Tessa raised an eyebrow. 'Any good?'

'Excellent, from what we heard.'

Well, it sounded as though Luke Stretton was earning his keep already. Tessa linked her hands on the desktop. 'Think he'll fit in OK?'

'I can't see any reason why not. He did the rounds of the shifts yesterday. Had a coffee with us early on. Said he wanted to get to know the staff a.s.a.p.'

Well, at least that sounded hopeful. They completed handover and Drew left.

Tessa began slotting pens into her top pocket. If everyone appeared to like Dr Stretton, she wasn't going to be the odd one out. She'd meet him halfway. After all, it was better to try to work in harmony than have turmoil all over the shop. Make love, not war. Her mouth flattened in a wry smile. Perhaps she wouldn't go that far!

Quietly, she began pulling the logistics of the shift

together. She was Acting Charge for the duration of her earlies. Nothing new in that. She'd got used to popping in and out of senior roles just to get the work done. It had become the nature of things in rural hospitals.

She noted she had Gwyneth and Roz on her team. They were both reasonably new graduates. Tessa looked thoughtful, Roz would be OK but Gwyneth?

'Good morning, Sister.'

Ignoring the kick in her heart, Tessa looked up, meeting the senior registrar's gaze as coolly as she could. 'Dr Stretton. Hello, again.'

'It's Luke.' A dark brow arched tauntingly.

'Are you all settled in?' Almost defensively, Tessa held some paperwork against her chest as he sauntered into her office and parked himself against the window-ledge.

'Pretty much.'

'Had the tour?'

'Yesterday, thanks. And thanks again for your help on Saturday night. Much appreciated.'

'You're welcome.'

Well, that seemed to take care of their small talk. Matching decisive action to her thoughts, Tessa dropped her paperwork into the out-tray. She turned and felt awareness feather right up her backbone...

Morning light outlined his features, highlighting hair that wasn't black at all but a darkish auburn, floppy in that perfectly arranged way that indicated a superb cut. She bit back a grin, doubting whether the hairdressers of Cressbrook would be up to his standards.

'Something amusing you, Sister?'

'It's Tessa,' she fired back, mimicking his earlier comment. 'I was just wondering where you got your hair styled.'

His gaze widened a fraction, the hint of a disconcerted frown passing over his face.

His eyes were a moody blue. Tessa decided to do the whole inventory while she was about it. Nice ears and mouth. Teeth? She hadn't yet seen him smile but she'd guess they would be in the same pristine condition as his hair.

She blinked, her gaze dropping to the faint cleft in his chin. Sexy... She felt the tingle in her fingertips and hastily shoved them into the side pockets of her navy trousers.

'Seen all you need to?'

'Was I staring? Sorry.' Tessa dipped her head to check her watch, disgusted to hear the huskiness in her voice. She firmed it up, 'I have to get the shift under way. Just shout if you need anything.'

Luke's smile unfolded lazily. 'Cup of tea?'

Well, really! For a second she was too stunned to reply but then she snapped her gaze away. 'Hot water and teabags in the kitchen. Help yourself.' *And* she'd been right about the teeth.

She swept out.

In the midst of the early-morning rush hour, Tessa was conscious of Luke everywhere. At least he seemed willing to get involved, she decided fairly. He was even exerting extreme patience with Brad Metcalf.

Instinct told her it was shaping up to be a busy Monday. She'd just done a quick tour of the cubicles and checked their supply of IV fluids when the emergency phone rang.

As she scribbled details, Luke came up light-footedly behind her. Damn the man! Tessa pulled back involuntarily. He was like a prowling cheetah.

'Problem, Sister?'

'Workplace accident.' Tessa replace the phone. 'Building site twenty kilometres out of town. The patient is a thirty-year-old male, Matthew Shearer. A nail gun misfired. The nails gone right through his boot into the top of his foot.'

Luke winced. 'Ambulance bringing him in?'

'ETA thirty minutes.'

'Right.' Luke rubbed a finger across his forehead in concentration. 'For starters, let's get someone here from the fire service to cut the boot off. And I don't want any cowboys showing up. I need someone who knows what they're doing,' he said firmly, his tone allowing no argument. 'And would you alert Theatre, please? It sounds like a job for Tom Eckhardt,' he added, referring to the hospital's general surgeon. 'And we'll need a blood specimen and cross-match immediately on arrival. Got all that?'

Sir! Tessa felt like saluting. Her hackles rose and refused to be tamped down. She began dialling, making a small face at Luke's broad back as he strode towards one of the treatment rooms. Just because she chose to work in rural health, did he imagine she was some kind of ninny?

Suddenly she felt put on her mettle. She'd show him. But locating an experienced officer from the fire service proved difficult. Tessa blew out a breath of frustration, deciding the gods were definitely not on her side this Monday. At last she had everything co-ordinated and Tony Santino, a volunteer from the fire service, was on his way.

'Thank heavens,' she murmured. Her morning had been rough enough already. She didn't need any more of Luke Stretton's little barbed innuendos chipping away at her self-esteem.

CHAPTER TWO

TESSA had already briefed Gwyneth, privately dismayed that the young RN was showing no initiative at all. A and E was not the place to have to begin spoon-feeding one of her team. And there were limits to the amount of support she could be expected to give anyway.

There just wasn't time for it, for one thing.

'OK?' She forced out an encouraging smile and Gwyneth fell into step as they began moving quickly towards the ambulance bay.

As they turned the corner, Tessa caught her breath, disconcerted for reasons she couldn't explain. Luke Stretton was already in position, feet planted firmly apart, waiting.

He gave her the cool imitation of a smile. 'Right on time, I see.'

Tessa bristled and brought her chin up. She hoped he got the message.

'Morning, all.' Len Taylor, one of the senior officers, sprang lightly from the rear of the vehicle. 'Early customer for you.'

'Any problems on the way in, Len?' Luke moved to take a share of the weight and the injured man was gently transferred to a hospital trolley.

'Not as such, Doc. As you can see, he's a bit green round the gills, though. Brought his breakfast up. BP's a touch on the low side as well.'

Luke's gaze met Tessa's across the trolley and together they tracked to the injured man. He looked ghastly pale beneath his tan. His eyes were closed, a clammy perspiration beading his forehead, each breath sound ending on a little moan.

'Let's move it.' Luke's voice was clipped.

'Cubicle one is ready.' Tessa's response was crisply calm and suddenly, professionally, they were working as a well-oiled team.

'Let me know when you need me, Doc.' Tony Santino poked his head into the treatment room, his pouch of tools at the ready.

Luke's, lean, handsome features were taut in concentration. 'We'll need to stabilise him first, mate. Just hang on a tick, would you? How's the blood pressure, Sister?'

'Eight-five on fifty.' Tessa released the cuff.

'Pulse isn't brilliant either,' Luke confirmed. 'Let's get a temperature reading, please.'

Tessa snapped the probe onto the electronic thermometer, getting an instantaneous readout. 'Thirty-five point five.'

'Right.' Luke's mouth drew in. 'Let's get an IV in, stat. He needs fluids and immediate pain relief. Make it fifty milligrams of pethidine and ten of Maxolon to settle his guts down.'

Tessa handed the keys of the drugs cupboard to Gwyneth. 'Take someone with you to double-check, please.' Turning back to her patient, she gently pulled back the space blanket. There was no alert bracelet. 'Are you allergic to any drugs that you know of, Matthew?'

The patient's eyes fluttered open and closed. He licked his lips. 'Don't think so…'

A few minutes later the medication and saline drip were starting to do their work. Tessa breathed a sigh of relief. 'His colour's improving.' She gave Luke a guarded smile.

'Mmm.' He seemed distracted. 'Time to get that boot off, I think.'

The fire officer performed the task with speedy expertise. Producing the sharpest, thinnest knife Tessa had ever seen, he sliced through the elasticised sides of the boot and peeled back the heel. Two forward cuts opened up the front section of the boot.

'If you could just steady his leg here, Doc?' Everything seemed to turn to stillness as Tony finally eased the flapping pieces of leather away from Matthew Shearer's rapidly swelling foot. 'And there we are…'

'Well done.' Luke looked dispassionately at the damaged foot as Tessa cut through the patient's thick sock with her scissors. He shook his head, his mouth tightening. It's a wonder he didn't pass out, poor blighter. 'Right, someone get a portable X-ray unit down here, please. I don't want our patient moved unnecessarily just yet.'

At last Matthew Shearer was on his way to Theatre. Tessa breathed a sigh of relief. Perhaps now she could find a few minutes for her paperwork.

She began making her way back to her office, only to hear her name called before she'd got halfway. It was Gwyneth.

'I've put a patient in cubicle three.' Gwyneth nibbled the edge of her bottom lip. 'He, um, insisted I was to get you.'

Tessa raised an eyebrow. 'Does he have a name?'

'John Abbott.'

Tessa groaned inwardly. The man had no fixed address. He was a regular at Casualty and had a history of ailments as long as your arm. 'How does he seem?'

'Obviously feeling ill,' Gwyneth said thinly. 'And he smells.'

'So would you if you lived rough.' Tessa's patience almost snapped. Gwyneth's attitude was getting right under her skin and it wouldn't do at all. She heaved in a controlling breath. 'You'll find every casualty department has its share of odd customers, Gwyneth. What would you have us do, turn him out?'

The junior RN looked taken aback. 'No. I only meant—'

'I know what you meant,' Tessa cut in quietly. 'And this time I'll handle it. But come and see me before the shift ends and I'll fill you in about John. OK?'

'Yes, Sister.'

Tessa's brow rose at the other's formality. Had she come across as some kind of dragon lady? Tough. She hardened her resolve. 'Now, would you stay with our patient, please, while I get a doctor to look at him? Otherwise, he'll bolt.'

Gwyneth's nod was courteous but not enthusiastic.

Tessa hurried away. Without giving herself time to dissemble, she went in search of Luke Stretton.

She found the SR in the staffroom. 'I'd like to talk

to you about the patient in cube three,' she said without preamble.

Luke looked up from the water cooler. 'Fire away,' he responded smoothly, lifting his paper cup and swallowing most of its contents.

'John Abbott, no permanent address, aged about twenty-five.' Tessa began to fill him in with tight-lipped determination. 'He's a regular. A bit eccentric, I suppose. The police usually pick him up from a shop doorway or somewhere and drop him here. Or sometimes he just wanders in from the cold. We treat him for cuts and bruises, the odd chest infection. Give him a shower and a new set of clothes from the hospital thrift shop and send him off.'

Luke crumpled his cup and sent it flying toward a nearby bin. 'Drugs?'

'We've never detected any sign.'

'How's his mental state?'

'I believe he receives a pension of some kind.' Tessa lifted a shoulder. 'Someone from the Salvation Army has been his advocate and allowed him to use their hostel as an address for social security requirements but John's a law unto himself.'

'One of life's loners.' Luke tugged at his bottom lip thoughtfully.

'Well...he...kind of trusts *me*,' she explained unevenly, 'if not the system.'

He studied her in silence for a moment, then said, 'You're warning me not to stomp all over him, aren't you?'

'I'm just explaining how things are.'

'I see.' His blue gaze ran across her face and down to where the open neck of her shirt ended in creamy shadow. 'Then we'd best take a look at him, hadn't we?'

Luke's examination was thorough. He ran his stethoscope over the young man's chest and back, his mouth tightening. John's thin bush shirt and faded jeans looked as though they'd been slept in many times over.

'You a doctor?' John looked up owlishly.

The corners of Luke's mouth lifted in a wry grin. 'The badge here on my shirt pocket says I am.'

'You don't wear a white coat like the others.'

'Don't believe in 'em. Cough for me now, please, John.' Luke dipped his head, listening. 'And again. You've got a few rattles in there. Where are you living at the moment?'

'Got a shed at the back of Fred Wheatley's garage.'

'No running water, I take it.' Slowly and carefully, Luke began palpating the young man's stomach.

Tessa knew he'd be checking for any hardening that could indicate a serious problem with one or more of his internal organs. 'Did you come in off your own bat, today, John?' She stood beside Luke, her expression concerned.

John nodded, interlocking his hands so tightly his knuckles showed white. 'Felt foul.'

'When did you last eat?' Folding his stethoscope, Luke parked himself on the end of the treatment couch.

'Dunno.' John shrugged his thin shoulders. 'Haven't felt hungry.'

Or didn't have any money left for food, Tessa

thought grimly. And heaven knew what he did with his benefit. He certainly didn't pay rent anywhere.

'I'm going to keep you in, John.' Decisively, Luke began scribbling on the chart Tessa handed him. 'We'll need you on antibiotics to zap that chest infection before it turns nasty. I'd like to run a few tests as well, see if we can turn anything else up. Is that OK with you?' He clicked his pen and slid it back into his shirt pocket.

The young man bit his lips together. 'I guess…'

Tessa came in with an overbright smile. 'Hey, we do look after our patients in here, you know.'

'Right.' Luke got to his feet. He was still holding the medical chart. 'Sister, I'd like to glance over John's history, if that's all right. When you've things organised for him to go to the ward, would you come along to my office, please?'

Tessa quickly delegated John Abbott's care to one of the assistants in nursing. 'Take him along to the shower, please, Carly, and he'll need pyjamas. Dr Stretton wants him admitted to the medical ward for some tests.'

'No worries.' Carly complied cheerfully. 'And while I'm about it, I'll consign John's old clothes to the incinerator, shall I?'

Tessa grinned. 'Unless you want to take them home to wash?'

'Not likely!' Carly's head with its blonde spiked hairstyle went back in a laugh.

A few minutes later, Tessa knocked on Luke's door. At his grunted reply, she opened it and went in. His head was bent over John Abbott's notes.

'Have a seat, Tessa.' Without looking up, he waved her to a chair.

Her name on his tongue came out soft and husky, the sound running along her veins like quicksilver. Tessa swallowed a bit unevenly and perched on the edge of the chair at right angles to his desk.

'It doesn't appear John Abbot's ever had a complete medical review.' Luke tossed the notes to one side and sent her a quizzical look.

Possibly not. And it was hardly her fault. 'We've had a procession of locums here over the last twelve months,' she said defensively. 'None of them appeared to want to go any further than they had to. Especially with the John Abbotts of the world.'

'That's a rather cynical statement.'

'I'm one of the people on the ground,' she said pointedly. 'I'm telling it as I see it.'

There was a moment of awkward silence and a creak of leather as Luke leaned back in his chair and folded his arms. He glinted a frosty blue look at her. 'I hope you're not including me in that company?'

Tessa shrugged inwardly. She didn't know enough about him or his work habits to answer that. But she was honest enough to admit that what she'd seen to date had impressed her. 'You appear quite dedicated.'

His lip curled. 'Damned with faint praise.'

Tessa felt the edge of an odd kind of tension zing between them, the challenging gleam in his narrowed gaze making her ask impulsively, 'What are your conclusions about John, anyway?'

'I haven't reached any,' he responded with maddening arrogance. 'But that's not to say I don't have a few hunches. We'll get some blood and send it off and see if that turns up anything.'

'Like what?' Tessa wasn't about to be fobbed off like a first-year student.

A contained little smile played around Luke's mouth. 'Like hypothyroidism.'

Tessa frowned. Under-activity of the thyroid gland. 'That's more common in women, isn't it?'

Luke looked taken aback, as if he wasn't used to having his diagnoses questioned. 'Perhaps.' He gave the response guardedly, a touch of irritation hardening the corners of his mouth. 'But we can't take a narrow, gender-based view and not test for it. As a case in point, last year at St David's we diagnosed a young *man* of twenty with breast cancer.'

Tessa sucked in her breath. OK, so he thought he was a good diagnostician. 'If you're right, I guess it would explain John's lethargy to some extent,' she conceded.

'There were other pointers.' Luke warmed to his subject. 'His heart rate was quite slow, and his skin seemed as dry as old bones. Didn't you notice?'

Tessa dug her toes in. 'That could just be a result of the particularly cold winter we've had, his diet and his less than adequate living arrangements.' And why on earth was she engaging in this confrontational sparring at all? As the senior medical officer, Luke Stretton's toes were definitely not for treading on. 'But, of course, you're the doctor,' she allowed.

'I've written him up for an ultrasound as well.' Luke became businesslike again, his measured tone indicating he hadn't missed her self-deprecating little rider. Rather ceremoniously, he passed John Abbott's notes across to her. 'I take it we send our bloods off to Brisbane for testing?'

She nodded. 'The courier collects from the hospital and from the GPs' surgery each afternoon.' She made to get to her feet. 'Now, if there's nothing else…?'

'Hang on a minute, would you?' He raised a delaying hand. 'As you're the local around here, I wanted to run something past you.'

A little warily, Tessa sank back into her chair.

'Do you know anything about this company our chap with the injured foot works for?'

Frowning, Tessa scrolled through her memory. 'They're not a local firm. I believe they're called Coulter Constructions. They're carrying out some work at Rosevale. It's a heritage-listed property out of town a bit.'

'According to Matthew's wife, it's the third accident in as many weeks. She's very angry about the situation. It's going to be some while before her husband's fit for work again.'

'He'll be insured through workers' compensation.' Tessa was at a loss to know where he was coming from.

'That's hardly the point, Sister, if there are shonky work practices going on.' The drawled tone was little short of biting sarcasm.

Tessa bridled. 'Surely you're not suggesting I should make it *my* business?'

'No.' Luke looked away briefly. 'But I think I'm about to make it mine.'

* * *

It was well past two o'clock before Tessa found time for lunch.

She'd missed out on the hot food but gratefully accepted a plate of freshly made sandwiches instead.

She gave a little sigh and looked around the canteen. The place was depressingly deserted. Collecting her tray of sandwiches and coffee, she turned towards the outside deck with its canopy of canvas sails, deciding that was a much nicer option. At least she could breathe in some fresh air and look at the mountains while she ate.

She pulled a wry face. The day so far hadn't been without its complications and she needed to bulk up her energy levels to cope with the remainder of it. Taking a hurried step out onto the wooden deck, she stopped and froze.

She had company.

And thanks to all the saints in heaven, Luke Stretton had his back to her! Tessa felt her heart jolt against her ribs, her eyes tracking to the lone figure. Luke was sitting beside one of the outdoor tables, his legs stretched out in front of him, giving every impression of being engrossed in the purple-blue hills away in the distance.

Tessa swallowed the dryness in her throat. Starting a new job was never easy. Had he come out here to be alone, to recoup his mental energies? His body language was giving every impression he had. Her fingers tightened on the edges of her tray. Perhaps she should take the hint and just fade quietly back inside…

Luke tried to get a grip on his wayward thoughts. He was usually so focused in the course of his working day but Tessa O'Malley's green eyes with their tangle of dark lashes kept getting in the way. Her eyes and her sassy mouth! Sweet heaven, she was diverting.

He tipped his head back, feeling the filtered warmth of the sun through the canvas roof, letting his mind drift and giving free rein to a contemplative, crooked smile. He wouldn't mind some action in this dead-and-alive place. But would Tessa slap him down if he made a move on her? Perhaps he should give it some more thought. After all, if he messed things up, he could hardly ask for a transfer.

In a frustrated gesture he pushed his long fingers back through his hair, the action catching something in his peripheral vision. He snapped his head round, as if compelled, only to feel his heart go into free-fall. 'Tessa...'

'Hi.'

CHAPTER THREE

'COME to join me?' Luke struggled to find a neutral tone amongst the chaos of his thoughts.

'Sure, why not?' Tessa had no idea how her legs carried her across to his table. She placed her tray down and sank into the chair he'd eased away from the table with his boot.

'I'm not intruding on your space, am I?' Tessa peeled the cling wrap away from her sandwiches.

His blue eyes glinted. 'I suspect it's the other way round. I'm the new one here.'

'Well, we don't charge for the scenery.' Her eyes cast down, she took a bite of her wholemeal chicken and avocado sandwich. 'It's fantastic, isn't it?'

'From where I'm sitting it is,' he said boldly.

Tessa refused to rise to the bait. Instead, she removed the lid from her take-away coffee with painstaking slowness, shaking in sugar and stirring it. 'Save your breath, Doctor.'

'It's Luke.'

His voice was low, distracting her to places she knew she'd never go with him. Never.

'So you keep telling me.' He had the temerity to laugh and Tessa felt her cheeks heat uncomfortably. 'How have you found things so far?' she asked in a desperate attempt to get back on a professional footing.

'Oh, by asking around. And I use my eyes quite a

bit.' His grin unfolded lazily, his eyes crinkling at the edges.

Tessa glared at him, her eyes shooting sparks. 'Very droll.'

He held back laughter as she gave him a go-to-hell look. Damn, he could thrive on sparring with her. She was beautiful, full of spirit. Elusive? Certainly. Attainable? That was a question he had yet to get the answer to. The thought of the chase made his heart flip over, his body leap to life.

'Enjoy your lunch?' Tessa waved a hand towards his empty plate with its knife and fork neatly aligned across the centre.

He gave an exaggerated sigh. 'Small talk is it now, Tessa? But to answer your question, yes, I did enjoy my lunch. The grub is very good.'

'We've an excellent chef at the moment. Let's hope he stays for a while.'

'Getting ancillary staff is a problem?'

Tessa snorted inelegantly. 'Keeping them more like.'

'The hospital is reasonably new, isn't it?'

She looked at him a bit suspiciously. Wasn't he overdoing the small talk just marginally? She raised her cup and took a mouthful of her coffee. She'd go with the flow for the moment. 'It was resited here almost two years ago now. We're very proud of it.'

Luke spun his hands up behind his neck. 'Yes, I can see you would be.'

A little silence fell between them. Tessa, feeling way out of her depth, turned her head to break the sudden tension, her gaze reaching out towards the hills that ringed Cressbrook. She took a deep breath, enthralled all over again with their gentle grandeur. 'What are you going to do with your time off?' she asked abruptly.

Luke looked startled. 'I hadn't given it any thought.'

'But surely you'd like to see something of the countryside while you're here?'

His broad shoulders lifted in a shrug. 'What's to see?'

Tessa felt an unexpected spurt of irritation. Surely he was kidding? But on the other hand, as a big-city type, he probably wasn't. She gave an almost indiscernible shake of her head.

'What?'

'You, Dr Stretton.' She laughed, a shaky little effort without much humour. 'You need re-educating.'

'Fine with me.' A grin began and widened knowingly. 'When do we begin?'

Tessa burned inwardly at the teasing glint in his eyes. Her heart pounding, she picked up her coffee, taking a careful mouthful, a crazy idea forming in her mind. 'Do you have the weekend off?'

'I believe so.'

'I'm going out to my grandmother's farm on Sunday,' she told him, cringing at the huskiness in her voice. 'You're welcome to come along for the drive.'

What on earth had she done?

Tessa had felt her stomach twist and knot every time she'd thought about it. And now it was Friday and she still had no idea whether Luke intended accepting her invitation to the farm.

He hadn't had a chance to answer when she'd suggested it. He'd been bleeped, cutting short their lunch-break and their conversation. And Tessa felt it was nothing she could have casually brought up with him later. It would have looked as though she was chasing after him.

But she'd have to find out soon. She glanced at her watch and immediately her breathing felt tight. In a matter of a couple of hours she'd be off duty and gone from the hospital for her three-day break…

Damn the man! Had he forgotten? Perhaps he was hoping she had.

Beside her, the emergency phone rang, bringing her back to reality with a thud. Suddenly she had a legitimate reason to speak to Luke.

'Possible arrest coming into Resus. ETA six minutes. It's Janet Weekes. She manages one of the pubs in town. Cardiac history. The ambulance has given Anginine with nil effect.'

'We'll have to wing it, then.' Luke's voice was clipped. 'And hope we come up with the right answers. What about family? Anyone to be notified?'

'She's a widow, relatively new to Cressbrook. I'll chase it up.'

'No.' Luke was firm. 'Delegate to Roz. I want you scrubbed and ready to catheterise. If our patient is overloaded, we don't have a second to waste. Gwyneth?' He rounded on the junior RN. 'I want you involved here, please.'

Gwyneth's eyes went wide. 'Yes, Luke.'

'And as soon as our patient hits the deck, I want the monitor leads on, OK?'

'If Mrs Weekes arrests, you're number three, Gwyneth.' Tessa was scrubbing furiously.

Gwyneth looked agitatedly from one to the other. 'Three?'

'You'll write what drugs are being given on the whiteboard.' Tessa was patient. 'And help with the IV fluids.'

'You'll be fine.' Luke sent out a brief encouraging smile to the nurse.

Gwyneth nodded and began to get the intubation tray ready.

Then there was no time to think.

The ambulance backed up to the rear entrance, its door already opening.

'Be good, team.' Luke's words snapped out and Janet Weekes was wheeled rapidly into Resus.

'She's not looking great, Doc.' Len Taylor's face was grim.

Luke wasted no time in supposition. His hands moved like lightning, securing a tourniquet and IV in seconds. 'Give me sixty of Lasix,' he barked. 'IDC in now, please, Tessa. Let's make a dent in that fluid.'

Tessa's hands were deft and sure.

'Eureka,' Luke murmured, as the crippling fluid began draining away. 'Let's clamp it at eight hundred mil. Sixty of Lasix, please.'

'That's one-twenty of Lasix so far, Doctor.'

'Thanks, Gwyneth. Could you adjust the oxygen to full now, please?'

'Mrs Weekes—Janet?' Luke leaned closer to his patient. 'You're in hospital. Did you forget to take your medication today by any chance?'

Janet's eyes fluttered open. She nodded. 'So stupid…'

'That's OK.' Luke spoke gently. 'So long as we know, we can treat you. Try to relax and breathe into the mask.' He shot an enquiring look at Tessa. 'How's the BP doing, Sister?'

'One-sixty over a hundred. Pulse a hundred and ten, respiration thirty.'

Luke acknowledged her call with a little nod. So far so good, he thought.

'Mrs Weekes has a daughter in Brisbane.' Roz popped her head into the room. 'Want me to phone?'

'I'll do it.' Luke arched back, his gaze intense, his tone brooking no discussion.

Roz's raised eyebrows spoke volumes before she quietly withdrew.

Luke knew he'd been curt and he'd apologise later. But his gut feeling was telling him they weren't out of the woods yet. And until he had his patient's possible prognosis sorted, he didn't want to start spreading alarm, perhaps unnecessarily, amongst her family.

'Thanks, Gwyneth, I'll do that.' Tessa took the basin and sponge and began to wipe Janet's face. She looked so unwell, so clammy still… Trepidation ripped through Tessa and automatically she felt for a pulse. Nothing. 'Code blue!' She hit the arrest button. There was flurry outside and Brad Metcalf appeared.

Luke was calm. 'Will you intubate, please, Brad? And I need adrenalin ten here.'

Gwyneth snapped the prepared dose into his hand.

'And another ten. Any pulse?'

'No.' Tessa felt her nerves pull as tight as a bow string.

'Let's defib, then, please.'

'Charging.' Brad blew out a long breath.

A high density of silence filled the room, becoming almost tangible while the machine charged.

'Clear!' Luke discharged the paddles.

All eyes swung towards the monitor, as if willing their combined energies into their patient. No evidence of a pulse showed. Luke swore under his breath. 'Come on, dammit! Don't dare shut down on me! Clear!' He tried the paddles once more.

This time the trace blipped and staggered into a rhythm.

'OK, we've got her,' Luke confirmed. 'Well done, team.'

'You did really well today, Gwyneth.' Tessa was fulsome in her praise to the younger woman.

'Oh. Thanks, Tessa.' Gwyneth's gaze dropped modestly. They were putting the resus room back to rights, Janet Weekes having been transferred to the hospital's small IC unit. 'I've had doubts about working in A and E,' Gwyneth confessed, stuffing the used linen into a nearby laundry bag. 'But working with Luke is excellent. I mean, he's so professional, isn't he? And so nice with it.'

Oh, lord! Tessa was caught between irritation and impatience. Was she dealing with a crush here? Gwyneth's pretty blush seemed to indicate it.

'I thought I might invite him for a drink after work,' Gwyneth went on dreamily. 'After all, he doesn't know many people here...'

Luke and Gwyneth? Oh, really! Lips clamped, Tessa busied herself at the basin, scrubbing it to within an inch of its life.

'Like me to take the report now?' Gwyneth asked, as they made their way back to the nurses' station.

'Oh, is it that time already?' Tessa blinked at this suddenly helpful Gwyneth. But instead of feeling pleased that the junior RN was beginning to turn her attitude around, Tessa was decidedly miffed.

She'd done her very best for Gwyneth over the week, cutting her so much slack it was ridiculous. Now it was as though the nurse had been reborn—and all as a result of a few encouraging words from a man! At least that's how it appeared to Tessa anyway.

'Actually, that'd be a great help.' Tessa conjured up a mysterious little smile. 'I do have some personal arrangements I need to confirm with Luke before I leave.'

'OK...' Gwyneth's face reflected wide-eyed uncertainty. 'See you on Monday, then.'

'I'm on days off until Tuesday.' Tessa fluttered a nonchalant wave, before making her way briskly along the corridor to Luke's office. She felt faintly ashamed. What on earth had goaded her into that pathetic display of one-upmanship with Gwyneth? Her breath spun out on a jagged sigh as she knocked.

'Yes?' Luke clipped the phone back on its rest as Tessa popped her head around the door. 'What's up?' He beckoned her in and then lowered his hands to execute a little rat-a-tat on the edge of his desk.

'Just touching bases before I go off duty.' Tessa kept her eyes averted, taking the chair opposite him.

'Have you managed to contact Mrs Weekes's daughter?'

Luke nodded. 'Renee Mitchell. Should be here in a couple of hours. She had a young family so she had to do a bit of juggling to arrange child care before she could set off.'

'You're not considering transferring Janet to Brisbane, then?'

'I've spoken to her cardiologist.' Luke considered his fingertips for a moment. 'Providing there are no complications, we agreed Janet can be safely managed here. And if she's on the scene and able to keep in touch with her people at the pub, it will probably lessen her stress levels.'

And thereby hasten Janet's recovery. Looking across at him, Tessa gave a guarded smile, oddly boosted by the fact that, like her, Luke obviously believed in a holistic approach to medicine.

'Must be time to call it a day, surely?' Luke's mouth compressed for a moment, a dark tendril of hair curling onto his forehead as he bent to glance at his watch.

'Yes.' Tessa rose instantly to her feet. He was politely chucking her out. She swallowed hard, not believing the disappointment she felt.

A beat of silence.

'So…are we still on for Sunday?' In one fluid movement Luke swung off his chair, moving around the desk towards her, stopping just short of touching her.

Tessa gripped the back of her chair. 'I thought you'd forgotten.'

'I thought *you* had.' His voice was low, his blue gaze stroking her like a physical caress.

Tessa found she could hardly breathe, his proximity sending a warm rush of want to every part of her body. She pulled back. That way was madness.

Wasn't it?

'What time do you want me?' Luke's gaze was intense and Tessa suddenly felt wildly uncomfortable. She licked her lips. It was almost as though he'd divined her wayward thoughts.

'I'll, um, swing by the doctors' residence about nine-thirty, OK?'

'I'll look forward to it.'

'And we'll take my Jeep.' Back on reasonably safe ground, Tessa firmed her voice. 'I wouldn't trust that turbocharged vehicle of yours on some of our roads.'

Luke made an offended noise in his throat. 'I'll have you know, Sister O'Malley, that my car has excellent handling credentials.'

'Let's not tempt fate, hmm?' Tessa's chuckle was spontaneous, rich and warm. 'I'd hate you to ruin those snappy leather boots digging us out of a boghole somewhere.'

Why on earth was she allowing her emotions to be tied in knots like this? And over a man again.

Tessa blew out a calming breath, settling the rib-knit red top across the waistline of her jeans. For heaven's sake! She was merely taking Luke to the farm, nothing more!

Pushing her feet into her riding boots, she caught sight of her reflection in the mirror as she straightened. She bit her lip. Despite her avowal that she was being sensible, practical and level-headed about this day out with Luke, her flushed image was reflecting a wide-eyed vulnerability. At twenty-nine years of age, too! Get a grip, Tessa, she warned silently. You've been round this track once before, remember?

But, then again, Luke wasn't Will Carter, was he?

Right on nine-thirty, she pulled her Jeep into the forecourt of the doctors' residence, marvelling anew at the gracious façade of lacy fretwork and the wide, sweeping front verandah of the old colonial home.

Luke was already waiting, comfortably dressed in jeans and a navy cotton-knit jumper pushed up to his elbows. Raising a hand in greeting, he jogged easily down the stairs as she drew to a halt.

Tessa fluttered a wave, recognising the little spiral in her tummy as pure, unadulterated happiness.

In a matter of moments, Luke had thrown open the door, tossed his medical bag over onto the back seat and piled in beside her. Almost in slow motion he turned to look at her. A moment's hesitation, then a lazy smile and a nod of satisfaction. 'You look good in civvies. I knew you would.'

Tessa felt the whisper of his breath on her cheek and carefully, and without quite knowing why, she released her seat belt and they were face to face and very close.

And at that precise moment, in a somersault of certainty, she knew he was going to kiss her. As if in a dream, she lifted her mouth to receive it, a long, exquisite shiver of a kiss that twined through her body languidly like smoke haze, unfolding from the tips of her toes to the top of her head.

'Luke…' Her eyes were dazed as the kiss ended and he pulled away.

'That's the first time you've used my name.'

The huskiness in his voice curled round Tessa like the softest silk. 'Is it?'

'Mmm.' He gave a dry smile, stroking the back of his index finger lightly over the curve of her cheek and across her chin.

She lifted her hand and their fingers touched briefly.

There was a short silence then he laughed softly. 'This is a hell of a place to be doing this.'

'Oh…' Tessa had never been lost for words in her life but now she felt blank, oddly exposed. 'Sorry, I—'

'No.' Luke shook his head, reaching out and enclosing both her hands in his. 'Don't be embarrassed, Tessa. I'm not.' His mouth quirked at the corners. 'No one's likely to be up and about anyway. Apart from me, the entire household is made up of residents.'

Tessa gave free rein to a smile. 'I seem to remember that when they're not sleeping, they're partying.'

'Isn't that the truth?' he said ruefully.

She looked up at him, concern written in her gaze. 'Is it very awful for you, staying here? I mean, it has to be light years away from what you're used to.'

One dark brow flicked upwards. 'It won't be for ever.'

'Oh, are you looking for a flat?' Tessa removed her hand from his and bent to refasten her seat belt. 'Perhaps I can help?'

A fleeting frown touched his eyes. 'No, I'm not

looking for a flat. I meant, I'm only here for three months. Well, three months minus a week now,' he added cheerfully, making himself comfortable and looping the seat belt over his shoulder.

Tessa's heart plummeted and she looked away quickly. She'd almost gone in boots and all again. But thank heavens she still had time to pull back. And when Luke left, as he surely would, she would still be heart-whole and able to say it had been fun while it had lasted.

Why, then, she wondered bitterly, did the whole scenario have such a hollow ring?

A little while later, Luke said, 'You've gone very quiet, Tessa.'

She flicked him a smile that didn't quite reach her eyes. 'I don't talk *all* the time, you know. Besides, I need to concentrate on my driving.'

Luke reflected on the arterial blockade of cars on any given morning in the city and huffed drily, 'I imagine the native animals on the road might cut into your progress a bit.'

Tessa showed him the tip of her tongue. 'And in case you're wondering, it's about thirty kilometres to Half Moon,' she enlightened him, changing gears as they began the ascent up through the hills.

'I take it that's the name of your grandmother's property?'

'Mmm. The O'Malleys took up land at Cressbrook in the 1880s. Originally, they operated a sawmill. There were beautiful cedar forests here then. Del still has some handmade furniture that's come down through the family.'

'Del?'

'Delia O'Malley. I've never managed to call her grandmother.'

'So Del is your dad's mother,' Luke pursued doggedly.

'That's right.' Tessa flicked a long tangle of hair back over her shoulder. 'In later years the O'Malley brothers went their separate ways and diversified. Our branch went into farming but Dad's heart was never in it. He pulled out about ten years ago and went into business in Brisbane.

'Del and my grandfather tried to carry on but dairying's too labour-intensive without family involvement. And then when Granddad died it was impossible. Del swapped over to beef cattle and appointed a manager, Brendan North.'

She gave a stilted little laugh. 'So there you have it, Dr Stretton, the potted history of the O'Malleys.'

'Not quite.' Luke looked across at her and smiled. 'Do you have siblings?'

'There's just me,' she said lightly. And then her voice dropped almost musingly. 'Half Moon's the most special place in the world to me.'

'Then I'm flattered you want to take me there. You're very much at home here, aren't you?' Luke added thoughtfully.

'It nearly killed me when I had to go away to boarding school for my higher education,' she admitted frankly. 'And then, of course, I'd decided I wanted to enrol in nursing so it meant more years again in the city.'

'Where did you train?'

'St Anne's in Brisbane.' She made a small face. 'The nuns kept us on our toes.'

'It's always been a splendid teaching hospital, though.'

'Mmm. Where did you train?'

'At the Royal.' Luke's mouth moved wryly. 'Then I moved to Sydney. Had a couple of frantic years in A and E at St Vincent's. After that it was back to Brisbane where I managed to get a place on the surgical training programme at St David's.'

'Impressive.' Tessa swallowed and asked the question she'd dreaded asking. 'And after Cressbrook?'

He shot her a look from under half-closed lids. 'The States, hopefully, for more surgical training. I've a place at the Jewish hospital in Louisville.'

She'd jumped back into her shell again. Luke lifted his hand and stroked his bottom lip almost absently. What a complex personality this woman was. Bubbling over with life one minute, introspective and serious the next. But, hell, he wasn't about to worry her complexities to death. Just spending the day with her like this was so much more than he'd let himself hope for.

Tessa had begun to feel the freedom that getting out of town always gave her. Already her mind was running ahead, the call of the mountain gorge with its steep, rocky walls and the incredible view from the plateau finding an echo somewhere deep inside her.

And the day promised to be another gem.

'Do you ride, Luke?'

'Maybe I could get to like this.'

They'd spoken together. 'You first,' Luke said, as they looked at each other and laughed.

'I just wondered if you could ride.'

He looked warily at her. 'There was an equestrian centre attached to the high school I attended.'

Tessa rolled her eyes. 'Like that tells me anything. Come on, Luke, tell me.'

'I'm afraid.'

'Of horses?'

'No.' Luke pretended to shudder. 'Of you, Sister O'Malley. You won't make me ride, will you?'

'Idiot.' Tessa laughed softly. 'I suspect you can ride, and very well.'

Luke snorted. 'Except for the races, I haven't been near a horse in yonks.'

Tessa smiled mischievously. It was rather nice having the upper hand like this and she was enjoying the small dent in Luke Stretton's confidence. 'You never lose the knack. And I'll find you a mount with a sweet temperament,' she reassured him. 'Besides, horseback is the only way to see the special places on Half Moon.'

'Yeah, yeah.' He sounded unconvinced. 'Who'll fix me up if I fall off?'

'You won't fall off! You can ride a bicycle, can't you?'

'Of course I can ride a bike. What's that got to do with anything?'

'Just think of the horse as a bike without wheels.'

'The mind boggles,' Luke muttered.

CHAPTER FOUR

DELIA O'MALLEY looked like nobody's grandmother.

Luke blinked at her washed-out jeans and bright pink shirt. The lady had to be somewhere in her seventies but there was no look of the frail aged about her. She was petite, as slim as a girl with an unlined, interesting face and shrewd grey-green eyes that he suspected wouldn't miss a beat.

'Luke.' Her handshake was firm. 'You're very welcome. Tessa's told me all about you.'

'She has? That's interesting.'

Tessa turned away from the teasing glint in his eyes, squirming inwardly. 'Del, I merely told you Luke was doing a locum for us in A and E.'

'So you did, dear.' Del smiled brightly, stretching across to open the oven door. 'I've made scones for morning tea. And there's a fresh loaf for you to take back with you, Tess.'

'Oh, yummy.' Tessa planted a swift peck on her grandmother's cheek. 'You indulge me shamelessly. Now, are we going to be grand and take tea in the dining room?'

'Indeed we're not, missy,' Del tutted. 'I've already set up on the back verandah.'

Tessa gurgled a soft laugh. 'I'll just show Luke where to wash his hands, then. Sheppy jumped all over us on the way in.'

'Dogs are inclined to do that,' Del said matter-of-factly, hefting the singing kettle off the stove top. 'Tea in five minutes, mind?'

Tessa led Luke along the soft pine flooring of the hallway. 'Bathroom's just here,' she said, opening the door on the long, narrow room with its old-fashioned, lion-claw-foot bath under the lead-light window.

Seeing the bath's depth and width, Luke whistled softly. 'Now, that has definite possibilities!'

His eyes were gleaming and Tessa felt a soft wash of colour brush her cheeks. 'But rather large just for washing your hands, Doctor.' Giving him a prim little look, she reached up to the brass rack for a towel.

He laughed softly, turning on the tap over the handbasin. 'She's amazing, isn't she?'

Of course, he was speaking about Del. 'She is.' Tessa's look was soft.

'I can see a reflection of you in about forty years' time.' Luke's eyes flickered back to hers and the warmth in them made her own breath jerk in response.

'I'm taller,' she flannelled, watching the film of soap bubbles curl off his hands as he washed.

'And sassier.' Smiling teasingly, he dodged back from the basin and caught the towel she threw at him.

'I've asked Brendan to yard the horses for you.' Del refilled their teamugs.

'Oh, good.' Tessa licked a spot of strawberry jam from her top lip. She looked up at her grandmother. 'Who did he bring in, do you know?'

'Well, Ladybird for you, of course. But not knowing Luke's prowess—'

'Or lack of it,' Luke cut in repressively.

Tessa sent him a weighted look. 'I'm sure we'll find a horse you can ride.'

Del nodded. 'Personally, I don't think you could go past Uppity Lad.'

Luke's jaw dropped. 'That's a horse?'

'He's lovely.' Tessa stifled a giggle. 'Former racehorse with a nice mouth.'

Luke made a sound of disbelief in his throat. Picking up his mug, he looked drily at Tessa over its rim. 'You're enjoying this, aren't you?'

'Who, *moi*?' She tilted her head, regarding him serenely. 'Uppity is a dream. Go anywhere you want him to.'

Luke sighed extravagantly. 'I'm beginning to identify with the poor unfortunate beast already.'

'That was fantastic, Mrs O'Malley. Thank you.' Replete, Luke pushed himself back from the table.

'Luke and I'll take care of this,' Tessa insisted, shooing her grandmother off. 'Go and put your feet up. Oh, and I brought your English *Woman's Weekly* out from town, too.'

'Thank you, darling.' Del looked pleased. 'I'm following the serial and there's a knitting pattern I want to get started on as well.'

It took the two of them no time at all to clear the table and set the kitchen to rights. 'You're quite domesticated, I see.' Tessa gave Luke an upside-down smile.

Luke raised a dark brow. 'Did you doubt it?'

'I hadn't thought about it,' she responded airily, plucking the damp teatowel out of his hand and replacing it near the Aga to dry. 'Now, come on, Dr Stretton,' she ordered, a hand lightly at his elbow, 'let's get some fresh air into our lungs and blow the cobwebs away.

'This used to be the old dairy,' Tessa said a few minutes later, indicating the yard where a knot of friendly-looking horses raised their heads at the newcomers. Veering away, she opened the door of a shed, selecting several items of tack. 'This looks about your size.' She passed across a well-oiled leather saddle and hefted her own lighter one. She looked him up and down. 'Possibly we'll have to alter the irons.'

'The stirrup irons,' Luke clarified, bending his shoulders to the task and following her across to the enclosure.

'You're taller than anyone else around here.' Tessa shot him a dimpled smile over her shoulder. She anchored her saddle along the top rail of the yard for easy access and, taking the bridle, opened the gate and began calling softly to the satiny-smooth bay mare.

Entranced, Luke watched as she caught, bridled and saddled Ladybird easily and then surveyed the rest. 'Right, that's Uppity over there.' She indicated a lively-looking black gelding. Tessa clicked her fingers. 'Come on, boy.' He came to her and she saddled him up while Luke watched.

'I'm sure I'd be much safer pinning and plating someone's leg.' Luke's wry smile couldn't completely hide his apprehension.

Tessa's hand brushed his as she steadied Uppity while Luke adjusted the girth. She frowned. Was he really that uptight? She bit her lip, acknowledging the situation she'd set up. 'Look, if you'd rather leave this for another time…'

'No way.' Swinging determinedly into the saddle, he looked down on her from his newly elevated position astride his mount. 'Never let it be said that Luke Stretton wimped on a challenge.'

Tessa wrinkled her nose at him, before swinging lightly into Ladybird's saddle, deftly circling the mare to steady her.

'Where are we aiming for?' Admiration flickered in Luke's eyes as he watched Tessa, her akubra tipped rakishly forward and her hair cascading from it to her shoulders.

She flicked a hand towards the line of lacy willows. 'I thought we'd cross the creek and head on up to the plateau. The view's pretty special from there.'

They took off at a leisurely pace.

'You OK?' Tessa asked from time to time.

'Absolutely.' In fact, Luke couldn't believe the sheer exhilaration he felt, seeing things he'd never experienced before. Like just now, when they'd ridden over the crest of the hill and disturbed the mob of feeding grey wallabies. Alerted to the presence of humans, the quaint little animals were suddenly all flying legs and tails, almost colliding in their haste to leap away to the safety of the scrub.

And Tessa had been right. A wry smile lifted the corners of Luke's mouth. He hadn't lost the knack.

Spurred on by the lightness of his mood, he gathered up the reins. 'Fancy a canter?'

Seeing the challenging thrust of his chin, Tessa laughed delightedly. 'You're on!'

In perfect rhythm, they took off across the paddock, their horses' hooves churning a wake of green through the lush spring grasses.

They climbed higher and higher, until Tessa signalled she was about to stop, wheeling her mount to a halt halfway up the slope. Her eyes alight with pleasure, she looked down. 'Isn't that fabulous?'

Luke reined in his mount beside her, his gaze following hers to the expanse of the valley below, across the faint shimmer of the creek and beyond to the homestead nestling like a doll's house far away on the natural rise of the land.

'Yes, it is...' He closed his eyes, breathing in the woodsy tang of late morning air, tasting it, almost hearing it. 'What now?' Gently, he reached out and took her hand, turned it and pressed her palm to his lips.

'Back down to the creek, I think.' Tessa took a long breath, unobtrusively reclaiming her hand. 'We'll, um, spell the horses for a bit and then head home—if that's OK?'

Luke raised his gaze to the eastern rim of the cloudless sky. 'Sounds perfect.'

The horses were surefooted, picking their way carefully down the roughened cattle track to the creek. Dismounting, Tessa looped the reins around Ladybird's neck, setting her free to graze.

Somewhat guardedly, Luke followed her example.

'Are you sure they won't wander off and leave us stranded?' he asked.

'Not when they have one another for company.' Tessa threw off her hat and shook her hair. Bending down to the edge of the stream, she scooped up a handful of water and drank it thirstily.

'Is that safe?' Luke hunkered down beside her, his dark head very close to hers.

Tessa scoffed a laugh. 'Of course it's safe! It's running water, Luke. And look…' She pointed to where the creek trickled over some rocks. 'That's watercress. And it's lush and green—a sure sign there's no pollution.'

'OK, OK.' Luke held up a hand in retreat. 'Get off your high horse.'

Tessa chuckled. 'I thought I just did.' Eyes gleaming with anticipation, she watched him dip his hand into the cool running water and gingerly hold the liquid to his mouth.

'Not bad.' He gave qualified approval.

'Not bad!' Tessa pretended outrage. 'It's wonderful! And far cleaner than that treated stuff you call water in the city—' She broke off, laughing. 'Luke! What are you doing?'

'Who, *moi*?' He grinned innocently, in the same instant showering her with a spray of water he'd scooped up from the creek.

'You rat!' Recklessly, she showered him back until it was a free-for-all battle between them.

'Enough!' Luke finally called a halt, the last of his ammunition slipping between his fingers in a silver rainbow of trickles.

'I'm drenched!' Tessa wailed, peeling her damp shirt away from the waistband of her jeans.

'Poor baby.' Luke grinned, quite unabashed. 'Come here. I'll warm you up.'

It seemed to Tessa that everything began happening in slow motion and in what followed there was no component of choice—only a kind of destiny.

Luke took her in his arms and she was suddenly, vibrantly aware of him, fluttering her eyes closed as he cradled her head and began to explore her face with his fingers. His fingertips idled, taking their time, delicate like the finest strands of silk. And when they reached her lips she parted them, in thrall to their exquisite touch which was sending shock waves right throughout her body.

'Tessa...open your eyes for me...'

She did, every part of her aware of the heat of his body against hers, of that fathomless blue gaze and of a need as basic as her own.

Moving fractionally away, Luke put his hands to her elbows, smoothing them up inside the sleeves of her T-shirt to enclose her upper arms.

A jagged breath left Tessa's mouth. She felt her skin prickle and then contract. She knew she should pull away, stop him in his tracks. He'd made it clear he was just passing through.

But they were in too deep now, alight for one another. The slight, convulsive movement from Luke was her undoing. Lifting her hands to the back of his neck, she gusted a tiny sound and drew his face down to hers.

And when they kissed, it seemed to her she was

coming home, that somehow she had always known the taste and feel of this man, the rightness of it all.

As if in a dream, she went with him as he gently lowered them to the grassy bank of the creek. 'Tess…you're beautiful…' He buried his face in her throat, his hands sliding beneath her T-shirt to roam restlessly across her back and then to her midriff, half circling her ribcage, driving upwards until his thumbs stroked the soft underswell of her breasts.

With a passion she hardly knew she possessed, Tessa kissed him back, opening her mouth on his, tasting him all over again.

How long they stayed wrapped in their own world she had no idea, but when he drew back, and they moved apart a little to look at one another, she could tell the sun had shifted. She swallowed. 'How—how long have we been here?'

Luke shook his head. He felt poleaxed, set adrift without a lifeline. 'Does it matter?' As if still compelled to touch her, he ran his hands down her arms to lace her fingers in his. 'Are you OK?'

What was OK anymore? The sunlight splintered Tessa's green eyes into tiny shards of gold as she reached out, stroking across the indentation of his chin and down his throat.

'Tess…' He leaned forward and found her mouth again with an urgency that matched his own.

A long time later, Tessa broke away and pulled back from him, breathing hard, as if fearful of her own response and where it would inevitably lead them, amazed that it hadn't already… 'Luke…' She jackknifed upright, straightening her shirt and refastening the top of her jeans. 'We should make tracks. Del will be wondering where we've got to.'

Luke was watching her, his gaze narrowed and assessing. 'And where have we got to, Tess?' he asked quietly.

She drew in a shallow breath, blinking at his wilful misunderstanding. Was he issuing a deliberate challenge? At the possibility, she felt her nerve-ends shred.

Blindly, she looked around for her hat and, finding it, jammed it on her head. The horses, she was relieved to see, had merely taken themselves off into the shade of a nearby stand of she-oaks.

As they made their way back to the house a few minutes later, Luke realised the contact was broken. Somewhere between the creek and the stable yards she'd mentally backed away from him. He didn't like it, but on the other hand he knew that to presume anything where Tessa O'Malley was concerned would be a mistake.

Tessa felt lost in confusion and a welter of unfamiliar emotions. Distancing herself from him was the only way she knew to shield her vulnerability. She couldn't think about the rest of the day or even tomorrow—let alone the future.

What future? He was going away…

Her jaw clenched as they walked along the back verandah towards the kitchen. Please, heaven, Del was having her usual afternoon nap otherwise she and Luke would be in for a very forthright inspection from those wise, grandmotherly eyes.

'Thanks.' Tessa dropped her gaze as Luke held the screen door open for her. 'I'll rustle up some food.'

There was a moment of awkward silence and then Luke cleared his throat. 'Would you rather skip the food and head straight back to town?'

Tessa returned tightly, 'That's not necessary. Surely you're hungry?'

Luke took her gently by the shoulders. 'Why are you suddenly so out of sync with me? What have I done?'

'Nothing.' Tessa's heart was suddenly hammering in her chest. If he was so insensitive not to recognise that what they'd done had altered everything between them, she wasn't about to tell him. She shrugged out from under his hands. 'I'll just check on Del.' She turned towards the hallway.

Delia wasn't in her bedroom. Tessa listened for the soft murmur of the television but the lounge room too was silent. Faint stirrings of unease gripped her and she went quickly from room to room. Nothing. No sign of her grandmother.

'Luke!' Almost running, Tessa retraced her steps along the hallway to the kitchen.

'What's up?' Luke turned from filling the kettle at the sink.

'I can't find Del!'

In one fluid movement Luke replaced the kettle on the stove top. 'Where would she normally be?'

Tessa's hand fisted agitatedly against her chest. 'Taking a nap or watching TV, but I can't find her anywhere in the house.'

'Perhaps she's outside,' Luke suggested logically.

'Of course!' Tessa looked as though she'd been thrown a lifeline. 'She'll be feeding the chickens…' She took off at a run.

'Hang on.' Luke caught the screen door before it slammed in his face. 'I'll come with you.'

The hens were in their run, scratching and clucking contentedly, but one glance told Tessa her grandmother was nowhere about. She turned to Luke, a blade-sharp panic in her eyes.

'Could she have gone out somewhere?' Luke's voice was calm but he acknowledged an uneasy feeling.

Tessa shook her head. 'Not without leaving a note—and she knows I'm usually not more than an hour or so when I go riding—'

Except today with Luke, she'd been much longer than an hour…

'Stop it, Tessa.' Luke homed in exactly on her scrambled thoughts. 'This is way beyond what you and I might have done or not done,' he added with deadly emphasis. 'And dragging it into the equation certainly isn't helping to find your grandmother. Now, you take the vegetable garden and that big clump of shrubbery at the side, and I'll take the orchard. Yell if you find anything.'

It was Luke who found Delia O'Malley.

Tessa heard his shout just as she made her way out of the patch of straggly corn at the bottom edge of the vegetable garden. She began running up the slight incline towards the orchard as if her life depended on it.

Luke knew this was not the moment to lose his professionalism but why today of all days had fate chosen to be so unkind? As if Tessa needed this emotional trip on top of everything else. And rightly or wrongly, she'd blame him. He just knew it.

Her little cry of distress as she jerked to a halt and dropped beside the prone figure of her grandmother tore at Luke's heart. 'Oh, my God!' She took Del's hand and held it tightly. 'Luke?' She threw a frantic look at him. 'She's not…?'

'Of course she's not, Tessa. Get a grip on yourself and help me.' Luke knew he was being harsh but to get the best for Del he had to goad her granddaughter into action. 'She's obviously been up on that ladder, trying to pick oranges from the high branches. Somehow she's lost her balance and fallen heavily. From my very cursory examination, it looks like a fractured NOF.'

Neck of femur. Tessa bit her lips together to stop them trembling. Immediately, she could see the irregularity of her grandmother's left leg, fractionally shorter than the right and now sitting painfully out of joint. She drew in a hard, controlling breath. 'It's…very serious at Del's age, isn't it?'

'It can be, yes.' Luke agreed. They both knew the resultant blood loss from such a severe break could prove fatal, especially to an older person. He placed his hand firmly on Tessa's wrist. 'There's no time to lose, Tess. I want you to phone for an ambulance and bring my bag. And blankets!' he shouted after her.

Del murmured incoherently, her restive movements alerting Luke. Frowning, he placed his fingers on her pulse, not surprised to find it weak and irregular. His mouth drew in. Her oxygen saturation would have to be low, too. But they couldn't do much about that until the ambulance arrived. 'You'll be OK, Del.'' Gently, he brushed the fine silver hair back from her forehead. 'Trust me...'

Luke felt the weight of responsibility almost cripple him. He thought of Tessa, so pale, holding herself together by a thread. Her grandmother meant the world to her. He wouldn't let either of them down if he could help it. But, sweet heaven, all his instincts were telling him that Delia O'Malley was in for a bumpy ride.

His mouth moved into a grim little twist. Perhaps he'd do better to just pray for a miracle.

'The ambulance will be here in twenty-five minutes.' Breathless, Tessa was back with blankets and a pillow.

Luke whistled under his breath. 'That's caning it.'

'The guys know these roads like the backs of their hands.' Gently, Tessa raised her grandmother's head, while Luke slid the pillow into place.

'And it's not like there's any traffic.'

Tessa's mouth wobbled. She knew Luke was talking generalities to take her mind off things. She'd done it a thousand times with patients' relatives. 'Here's your bag.'

'Do you know if Del's on any medication?' Luke shot open the locks on his medical bag.

Tessa felt suddenly at a loss. 'She's not said anything—but she's pretty cagey about all that stuff. What are you giving her?'

His jaw tightened. 'I'm going with morphine five milligrams and Maxolon, of course, to combat any nausea, but I'd be happier if I knew some history. Who's her GP?'

'She's had the same one for years—Denis Mulchay.'

'Then get him on the phone, please.'

'But it's Sunday!' Tessa was all but wringing her hands.

'I don't care if it's bloody pancake day!' Luke sent the painkiller home. 'Do I have to spell it out, Tessa? Get on to him! He'll have an answering service, for crying out loud.'

For a second Tessa stared at Luke in numb disbelief and then she exploded into a run.

Several minutes later she was back. 'I located Dr Mulchay at the golf club.' Her breathing was shallow, her heart beating like a drum. One hand on her chest, she took a moment to compose herself. 'He…said he's prescribed digoxin for Del.'

The medication was used to strengthen the action of the heart. Luke's eyes narrowed in conjecture. With that kind of history, perhaps Del had become giddy. It would explain her fall. 'Right. At least that gives us something to work on. Well done, Tess.'

Tessa dropped once more to her grandmother's side. She shook her head. She felt confused, angry, sick with trepidation. 'S-she's never said anything, Luke. Not a word.'

Luke could hardly bear to watch her grief. 'I know it's an old chestnut, Tessa, but she probably didn't want to worry you.'

'But I'm a nurse! And her *granddaughter*, for heaven's sake!' Her voice cracked and she clamped her lips hard, struggling with her tumbled emotions.

Luke shook his head in frustration, wishing with all that was in him that he could do something to comfort her. He put a hand on her shoulder and squeezed and then they heard it together. The long wail of the ambulance siren.

Luke asked quietly, 'Are you OK to direct them?'

Tessa nodded, blinking back tears and stumbling to her feet. 'Len Taylor's on his own. I'll, um, tell him to back up as close as he c-can.'

Within seconds of the ambulance's arrival, Luke was issuing orders. 'Let's get our patient on oxygen. Tessa, will you monitor her, please?' He turned to the ambulance officer. 'Mrs O'Malley needs fluids, Len. We'll run haemacell, stat.'

'Right you are, Doc. I'll hook up the heart monitor as well.'

'Good man.' Luke's hands moved like lightning to secure a line to receive the IV fluids. 'How're her oxygen sats, Tessa?'

'Low.' Tessa's face was tightly controlled. 'Eighty-nine per cent.'

Luke scrubbed a hand across his cheekbones. He wasn't surprised. But he was placing his bets on the heart monitor telling him more. Seconds later his suspicions were confirmed. Del was showing every sign of being in atrial fibrilation. And although that didn't mean her condition was life-threatening, she was certainly very ill.

He'd make a more in-depth investigation when they got her to Resus. It was possible she'd need a digoxin boost. If it was indicated, the drug could be introduced very carefully through an IV.

Del had begun to come round but, despite Tessa's soft reassurances, the elderly woman seemed confused and unhappy.

Luke tried to keep a professional distance, knowing it was the only way they could hope to get through the next few hours. He said brusquely, 'We have to expect it, Tessa.'

She glared at him. She knew that but it didn't make it any easier to bear. 'Will you accompany her in the ambulance?'

Luke's head went back. She'd said it almost accusingly. 'Of course. Now, we'd better move.' He turned to speak to Len. 'Get on to the hospital, please, Len. Give them an ETA and tell them we're bringing Mrs O'Malley in for surgery. I'll scrub, and if they could round up at least two experienced theatre nurses, I'd be grateful.'

'No worries, Doc.' Len vaulted out of the ambulance and hurried round to the front cabin. He recognised the voice of authority when he heard it.

Luke expelled a hard breath. 'Tessa, listen to me,' he began, his voice low. 'I realise you'd prefer to be the one to travel with Del, but I promise to take great care of her, all right?'

She nodded mutely. Deep down she knew he would. But would it be enough? Luke Stretton wasn't God—no surgeon, however brilliant, was. And there were still terrible risks associated with surgery of any kind. And with someone of her grandmother's age…

'I've the animals to see to anyway,' she said, her voice defensive, muffled with emotion. 'And I'll have to phone Brendan.' She caught her lower lip and swallowed. 'I'll pack a bag for Del, and bring it in to the hospital…'

Luke's jaw clenched. She looked so desolate, her

shoulders hunched against her misery. He wanted simply to hold her.

But now was not the time. And perhaps it never would be, he thought starkly.

There was a long moment of silence, then Luke pulled the rear doors of the ambulance closed.

Tessa stayed motionless, a solitary figure, watching the vehicle gather speed, its shape dwindle, until it was lost in the blue-green haze of the eucalypts along the bush track.

CHAPTER FIVE

It was seven o'clock that evening before Tessa saw Luke again.

When he'd left in the ambulance, she'd done what had needed doing, finally returning indoors to pack for Del, gathering up her nighties and dressing-gown, her toiletry items and the soft lawn handkerchiefs she favoured over tissues. Tessa had brought the little case to the hospital and had handed it over to Benita Cohen, the charge on surgical.

Taking the suitcase, Benita said kindly, 'Tessa, your grandmother won't be down for a while. Emergency Caesar took precedence. Luke made himself useful.'

Tessa drummed up the ghost of a dry smile. 'He's supposed to be off duty today.'

Benita huffed. 'When did that ever cut any ice in rural medicine?'

Now knowing what else to do, Tessa wandered aimlessly to A and E. It was almost her home away from home, she thought bleakly, and she'd never felt so lonely in her life.

'Hey, you're supposed to be on days off.' Sue, who had been called in as replacement charge, popped her head into the staffroom.

'Hi.' Tessa was propped at the table, an out-of-date magazine and her third cup of coffee in front of her. There was a little catch in her voice as she poured out the circumstances of Del's accident.

'What a terrible thing to happen,' Sue commiserated, coming into the room. 'Honey, I'm so sorry. But your gran's in safe hands with Luke.' She looked thoughtful. 'Be nice if we could think of some way to get him to stay on, wouldn't it?'

'He's committed elsewhere.'

'Really?' Sue exclaimed curiously. 'He's talked to you about it, then?'

'In passing.' Just as she was wishing belatedly she'd kept her mouth closed, Tessa looked up to see Luke, still in theatre scrubs, push through the louvred doors into the staffroom.

Her stomach twisted at his grave demeanour. 'H-how is she? I asked Theatre to ring me here when—'

'I decided to come myself,' Luke broke in.

'And?'

'Everything went well. Del's in Recovery.'

'Oh…' Tessa's voice cracked and she realised how inadequate that sounded. 'I'd better get up there.'

'Give it a minute, Tess.' Luke rubbed a hand across his jaw. 'I want to talk to you.'

Sue's gaze flicked between them. Suddenly, her antennae were twitching. Heavens, she must have been going around with her eyes closed. The chemistry between these two was almost combustible. She made a move towards the door. 'I'll leave you to it, then, guys,' she said calmly. 'Yell if you need me to do anything.'

As if they were choreographed, their eyes followed

the charge as she left and then, as if they had nowhere else to go, went back to each other and locked.

Finally, Luke looked away, breaking the tension. Lifting a hand, he dragged it through his hair, leaving several strands free to bounce back on his forehead. 'Any chance I could grab a coffee?' He pulled out a chair and sat down.

Suddenly Tessa felt riddled with guilt. He must be out on his feet. And he'd probably had nothing to eat since their morning tea at Half Moon.

She made fresh coffee as quickly as she could and opened a tin of assorted sweet biscuits and placed everything in front of him.

Luke frowned. 'You're not having one?'

'I'm all coffeed out, I think.' Tessa lifted a shoulder indifferently.

'Del's looking good.' Luke dipped into the tin of biscuits, taking a handful. 'I took what I considered the best option and gave her a Richards pin and plate.'

Tessa nodded, familiar with the procedure which, put simply, meant Luke had screwed and plated Del's thigh bone together again.

'I don't need to tell you that, post-op, she'll possibly still be a bit confused but that should reverse in a day or so. All going well, I'd like her up on day two to begin some physio on a rollator.'

That soon. Luke must be very confident about her grandmother's full recovery. Tessa's shoulders sagged with relief. 'She'll need three or four weeks rehab, won't she?'

'Obviously.'

A beat of silence. His eyes narrowed, Luke looked

at her over the rim of his mug. 'Did you get everything squared away at the farm?'

'Yes. I fed the chickens, and Sheppy and Brendan will be out early tomorrow to take over…'

'And what about you, Tessa?'

Her chin snapped up. 'What about me?'

'Are you OK?' Luke frowned. Of course she wasn't. She looked *haunted*—for want of a better word.

'I should have been there to gather the fruit for Del.' Her voice was low, anguished. 'I always do those jobs for her. *Always.* She depends on me. Instead, I was with you and…'

Luke's frown deepened. 'So, what are you saying, Tessa, that Del's accident was somehow my fault because I *delayed* you?'

Her breath caught and fire flooded her cheeks. His meaning was clear and her response was instinctive. 'No, of course I'm not, but you started it!'

'Started what?' His eyes were like flint with tiny silver shards.

'Everything!'

'I don't understand the implication of these words you're throwing at me, Tessa.' His moody blue eyes were fixed unflinchingly on hers.

'Then I'll spell it out for you.' Tessa fought for control of her wildly see-sawing heart. 'What happened between us at the creek shouldn't have happened—'

'Don't give me that! We both wanted it to happen.' A growl of disgust left his throat. 'What century are you living in, Tessa?'

'I won't get involved with you, Luke.'

His jaw tightened. Her voice had a husky determination in it and he had the unnerving feeling of being on stage without a script. He took a breath so deep it hurt. 'On the other hand, if you could bring yourself to trust a little, we could have something wonderful together.'

'And in three months you're gone!' Her eyes flashed with bitterness. She'd been down that road before.

In the silence that followed, Luke reached across and took her hand, unfolding her clenched fingers one by one. The action seemed to go on for ever, bringing Tessa very close to the edge. Suddenly, without warning, she felt surrounded by him, his masculine strength and the wild pull he exerted on every one of her senses.

'Tessa…'

'No, Luke.' Her voice was fainter than air.

'We *could* have something wonderful,' he repeated quietly.

Or be on the road to heartbreak. She shook her head.

'I'll back off, then.' Luke felt as though there were hands on his heart, slowly twisting the life from it. 'If that's what you want.'

What did she want? Shakenly, she realised that what she most wanted she couldn't have. The timing was all wrong for her and Luke. She swallowed the razor-sharp emotion clogging her throat. 'That's what I want.'

There was no chance of avoiding him indefinitely.

In the hope she might do exactly that, Tessa delayed her visit to Del on Monday morning, thinking Luke would have already made an early round. He had, but he was back again. She heard him tossing a cheerful greeting around the ward and then stopping by the door of Del's room.

He came in, nodded a greeting and picked up the chart, his mouth compressing as he made several alterations. Replacing the chart, he looked up and pocketed his pen. 'Tessa, I'd like a word before you leave, if you don't mind?'

Tessa felt a tiny seed of anxiety spring from nowhere. Was there some repercussion from Del's surgery he wanted to tell her about? Or worse? She swallowed. 'OK—your office?'

Luke glanced at his watch and frowned. 'Make it the cafeteria. I'm due for a break. Ten minutes?'

Tessa nodded.

Coming into the canteen, she immediately picked out Luke's distinctive head at the top of the queue.

He acknowledged her with a token smile. 'I ordered for you as well. Toasted sandwiches all right? Thought you might have skipped breakfast.' And there was no doubt she'd missed sleep. He swore silently. He'd done no better, almost pounding his pillow into a pulp before forcing himself into a sleep that had brought no peace and no answers.

As if by silent, mutual consent, they made their way out onto the deck. When they were seated, Tessa poured their tea from the rather battered stainless-steel teapot.

'Thanks.' Luke took his cup. 'I've been hanging out for this.'

Tessa couldn't look at him. 'I didn't get round to

eating breakfast either. What did you want to see me about?' She raised her head, burying her hands on her lap, digging her nails into her palms. 'Is it Del?'

'She's come through the anaesthetic better than I expected and physically her prognosis is good.'

Tessa swallowed drily. 'So, what are you saying?'

Luke lifted his cup and took a mouthful of tea. 'I was called in this morning about five. Del was very fretful, worrying about everything under the sun but mostly about you.'

They looked at each other and Tessa grimaced. 'I've just spent the last hour reassuring her I haven't fallen to pieces and that she's the one we have to be concerned about. I thought she'd settled quite nicely. At least for the moment. But I realise it's going to be a long haul and, of course, I want to be there for her—'

'What about your parents?' Luke broke in. 'Are they going to be able to help with her convalescence?'

'They're overseas. Their first holiday in years. I managed to call them last night. They're due home in a few weeks anyway. And, yes, I'm sure they'll want to take Del back to Brisbane with them after the rehab.'

'But will Del want to go?' Luke wondered aloud.

Tessa frowned. Oh, lord. Well, they'd just have to cross that bridge when they came to it.

'When are you back on duty?' Luke asked the question as uninterestedly as if she'd been the merest acquaintance. He'd returned their tray to the kitchen staff and they were making their way back through Reception.

Tessa nibbled her bottom lip. 'Tomorrow, on an early.'

'Catch up with you later, then.' Lifting a hand in the briefest farewell, he strode off towards the A and E department.

Well, what did you expect, brass bands? Tessa railed, watching him go and hating herself for her self-pity. He was only doing what she'd asked him to do. Backing off.

She went to work next morning, her heart as heavy as lead. The first sight to greet her on the ward was the tableau of Luke and Gwyneth, their heads together in earnest conversation.

Tessa's lips compressed. She felt like throwing things. Instead, she silently called Luke a traitor and then, scraping up all her inner resources, went to take the report. She was acting charge again.

At least in Casualty there was no time to go around feeling sorry for yourself, Tessa thought. She'd put Gwyneth on triage and was working with Roz herself.

'How's your gran?' Roz asked, as they sorted the sterile supplies together.

'As well as can be expected.' Tessa gave the standard hospital reply and Roz chuckled. 'Seriously,' Tessa went on, 'she's picked up pretty well. Luke's hopeful of getting her mobile as early as today.'

Roz laughed softly. 'He's a babe, isn't he? Or as my nan would say, "a bit of all right". And practical with it. Makes facilitating an art form. Best senior reg. I've worked with anyway. Oh, I'll find a home for these, shall I?' Scooping up a bundle of sheepskins that had come in from the laundry, she ducked off into a nearby utility room.

While Tessa was still digesting Roz's flattering litany on Luke, the man himself shoved his head around the door. 'Morning, Tessa. I'll be in my office if you need me.'

Tessa's heart hitched to a halt. She opened her mouth but he was gone again before she'd had time to answer. Her spirits drooped. So, it was to be business as usual.

Well, isn't that what you wanted? the smug voice of reason infiltrated craftily. Of course it was! Then why, she wondered bleakly, was her heart so filled with doubts?

Midmorning, Gwyneth came hurrying to find Tessa. 'I think someone should see this patient right away.'

'What's the problem?' Tessa dropped what she was doing to accompany the junior sister back to the waiting area.

'He's been mauled by dogs.' Gwyneth's small pert nose wrinkled in distaste. 'It looks *gross*.'

Tessa clamped her mouth shut.

The injured man was Doug Tanner, a council worker. His foreman, Max Evans, had brought him to the hospital after the dog attack. He greeted Tessa with a curt little nod. 'The council's gonna have to consider tougher dog-control laws after this lot, Sister.'

And probably not before time. Instantly, Tessa could see that Doug was in considerable shock and no wonder. Poor man. Both his arm and leg had been viciously mauled. And he'd been wearing shorts, which hadn't helped. 'Right, Doug, let's get you into a treatment room and make you more comfortable, shall we? Get a wheelchair, please, Gwyneth.' Tessa directed, halting the man's efforts to get to his feet.

'Should I wait, Sister?' The foreman looked on in concern, turning the broad brim of his hat in his hands. 'Or I could let his wife know...'

Tessa shook her head. 'That's kind of you, Mr Evans, but we'll do that, and it's really not necessary for you to wait. Give us a call in a couple of hours. We should be able to give you an update on Doug by then.'

Leaving Gwyneth to gather Doug Tanner's relevant details, Tessa went to find Luke, succeeding in tracking him down in his office. 'Fancy a bit of suturing?' she asked without preamble, and proceeded to fill him in.

In the treatment room, Luke made a thorough examination of Doug's wounds. His mouth compressed. There were severe bites to his right forearm and ugly puncture and tear marks to his left leg. 'Hells bells,' he growled. 'They didn't miss you, mate. What breed were they?'

'Big.' Doug attempted a cracked laugh. 'And bloomin' savage. Hell, Doc, I thought I was a gonner there for a while...'

'How did it happen?' Luke went to the basin to wash his hands.

'I drive a grader for the council,' the man explained. 'We're doing a bit of work just on the fringe of town. I left the grader to use the portable loo, see. And I noticed these mongrel dogs rummaging through a rubbish bin, draggin' stuff all over the place. I chased 'em off and turned round to go into the loo and then they were on me.' He shook his head, as though still in disbelief.

'That's frightening,' Tessa breathed. 'Did you call for help?'

'Yeah. And lucky for me, Max was only up the road a bit. He heard me yell.'

'And obviously came to your aid,' Luke said, folding his arms and looking down almost in admiration at the injured man.

Doug gave a half-grin. 'Beat 'em off with a shovel.'

Tessa shuddered. The treacherous animals would, no doubt, have to be caught and put down.

'Right, Sister.' Luke was immediately back in professional mode. 'Could you settle our patient into the small theatre, please? And I'll need you to assist.' He turned to Doug. 'I'll just get into some fancy clobber, mate, and we'll see about sorting you out.'

Tessa was already gowned and masked when Luke reappeared. She'd drawn up lignocaine and opened the suture packs.

'This'll sting a bit, Doug,' Luke apologised, infiltrating the patient's wounds with lignocaine. 'And you'll have to back up for a tetanus jab as well, I'm afraid.'

'No worries, Doc. Feels like a feather duster after those canine teeth tearing at me...'

Luke judged the anaesthetic had taken effect. 'Right, Sister, we'll clean and debride now. Would you take the arm, please, and I'll tackle the leg?'

Two hours later, Luke peeled off his gloves and stretched. 'That should do it, Doug. Come back in a week and we'll have a look at you. You should be able to have the majority of the sutures out then, or earlier if they're giving you any grief. Try to keep them dry and I'll give you a script for some antibiotics. Now...' he half turned and winked at Tessa '...I believe your wife's outside to take you home, isn't that so, Sister?'

Tessa nodded, smiling faintly. Luke was acting as though everything between them was all sweetness and light, when they both knew it wasn't. She swallowed unevenly. 'Mr Tanner will need a certificate for work, as well, if you wouldn't mind.'

Several minutes later, Luke returned with the medical certificate and script. 'If you need more time off, I'll organise another note when you're next here. In the meantime, any problems, come back to Casualty *pronto*.'

'Thanks, Doc.' Doug grimaced slightly as Tessa helped him into a wheelchair. 'Be seeing you.' He looked up over his shoulder. 'Do I really need to be in this thing, Sister?'

'Hospital rules, Doug,' Tessa said lightly, wheeling him along to Reception and handing him over to his wife.

Tessa glanced at her watch, considering whether to delegate someone to put the little theatre back to rights. Just as quickly she rejected the idea. They were short-staffed, and by the time she found somebody, she could probably have done it herself.

Sighing, she made her way back along the corridor and pushed the door open, startled to find Luke still there. He was peering out the window, massaging a tension point at the top of his spine. She faltered, almost tempted to tiptoe away, but he'd swung round and seen her. Her heart took a giant leap. 'Shoulder cramp?'

'Just a tad. Long old job,' he said ruefully.

Without stopping to allow herself to summon up a dozen excuses for what she was about to do, Tessa wheeled out one of the backless high stools and shoved it towards him. 'Sit.'

Luke eyed her suspiciously. 'To what end?'

'Your rear end,' Tessa said facetiously. 'Just sit, Luke. I'll have a go at getting rid of your muscle tension.'

Still looking baffled, he nevertheless did what he was told. 'Now what?'

'Hold your hands out, palms up.'

'Are we praying?'

Tessa gave a click of annoyance. 'It's called reflexology. Surely you've heard of it?'

Luke's eyebrows lifted sceptically. 'I've probably seen it written on a blackboard outside one of those alternative-lifestyle haunts.'

'Maybe it's time to open your mind, then. The nerves in the hand represent a map of the body,' she said knowledgeably. 'Some ailments can be relieved simply by touching or stimulating certain points.'

'Hmm...I like the sound of that.' He smiled and their eyes clashed and held.

Tessa looked away first, her heart dancing an unfamiliar jig of its own. 'Now, just relax, please, and let me try this.'

'This' was something called 'thumb walking'. Expertly, Tessa inched her thumb from the outer edge of Luke's palm to the tip of his thumb.

He looked on amusedly while she carried out the ritual three times on each of his hands. 'So, what is it supposedly doing for me?'

'This area represents the nerves running along your spine and vertebrae.'

'I see...'

'Now, I work your solar plexus point.' With her thumb and forefinger, she pinched the centre of his palm, working to a rhythm. 'Hopefully, this will induce muscle relaxation throughout your trunk and spine.'

'When did you learn all this?'

'Last year, when I was still living in Brisbane. I needed something to do with my evenings after...'

'After?' He tilted his head.

'After work,' she said too quickly, the set of her small chin almost defiant as she intercepted his doubting expression.

'And if I believed that, Tessa, I'd believe anything.'

'Is this beginning to work?'

'Not yet. But it feels nice,' he qualified.

Tessa faltered, recognising she was hopelessly out of her depth with him like this. She glanced up to see Luke staring at her. 'What?'

His eyes lifted to her hair. 'It looked like a wild river of black silk when you wore it down on Sunday. Felt like silk, too...'

Tessa froze, a sudden pulse of emotion flooding to the feminine core of her body. 'You're not playing fair, Luke,' she said thickly, finding it hard to breathe while he was watching her so intently. 'You said you'd back off.'

'So maybe I fudged a little.'

She pulled her hands away. 'That's all. Let me know if it works.'

Luke got slowly to his feet and placed the stool against the wall. 'Are you doing anything for lunch?'

'Actually, I thought I'd spend my break with Del.' Tessa's throat made a convulsive movement as she concentrated on the practicalities of clearing up from the operation. 'I want to see how her physio went.'

'I'd like to check on her progress myself. Shall we go up together?'

'Don't wait for me. I'll be a while yet,' Tessa said shortly. Damn the man! She felt as though she were being backed slowly and inexorably against a brick wall.

'I'll wait.' His mouth tightened, as if he'd guessed her thoughts. 'I want to grab a shower anyway. Give me a shout when you're free.'

Carrie Newman, the sister at the nurses' station on the surgical ward, met them with a smile. She pulled the notes and handed them to Luke. 'Mrs O'Malley's physio went well,' she reported. 'But knocked her right out, poor pet. She's asleep.'

'I'd still like to pop in on her.' Tessa was determined.

'Sure.' Carrie flapped a hand. 'You know the way.'

Softly, so as not to disturb her, Tessa opened the door to Del's little private room. Her expression tensed and all her guilt came tumbling back. Her grandmother looked so vulnerable. Reaching out, Tessa took Del's hand and held it, so engrossed she hardly noticed Luke slip in quietly.

With his head bent, he wrote something on the chart. And then he looked up and signalled that he was leaving.

Tessa nodded, breathing a sigh of relief which was short-lived. He was waiting for her when she came back to the station. They fell into step along the corridor. 'Are you pleased with her?'

He looked up sharply with a frown. 'Broadly speaking. She seems a little fragile but that's only to be expected. I've changed her pain medication but otherwise we'll let things progress as is.'

'I'll look in on her again after work.' Tessa tilted her head towards him. 'You would tell me if there was anything…untoward?'

Luke felt his gut contract. She looked as vulnerable as a kitten trapped on a high wire, her green eyes all soft and misty. 'Of course I would…' His jaw clenched and he noticed the way her gaze fluttered down, as if just conversing with him unnerved her.

'I really would tell you, Tess…' he heard himself insisting, at the same time wrapping his arm gently around her shoulders.

Hardly aware of what she was doing, Tessa let her head rest against him. 'I haven't even thanked you properly for what you did for Del.'

'I don't expect thanks.' He breathed in, absorbing her scent, so utterly aware of her and the reaction of his own body. He gave a cracked laugh. 'It's what I do, for Pete's sake.'

Her teeth bit softly into her lower lip. 'You've been so nice to me. I thought you might…well, I thought things between us might have been a bit awkward.'

'Hey, we're grown-ups, aren't we?' Abruptly, Luke brought them to a halt against the sunshine-yellow mural. A solemn light came into his eyes and he brushed the pad of his thumb against her cheek. 'I figure if I can't be your lover then I'd like to be your friend.'

Dazed, she watched the small lifting of his throat as he swallowed, feeling a surge of oneness with him, a burst of happiness she couldn't hide. She managed a tentative smile. 'And we don't have to make life-changing decisions right this minute, do we?'

'No.' Carefully, he scooped up a wayward tendril of her hair and tucked it behind her ear, his gaze tender. 'But first things first. You need feeding.'

The cafeteria was packed. 'The sausages and mash sounds good.' Luke craned his head higher to read the blackboard. 'Suit you?'

Tessa made a sound of dissension. 'How can you even contemplate eating that in the middle of the day?'

'Easily.' He grinned. 'Come on, Tess, join me—live a little.'

'That's exactly what I intend to do,' she responded rather primly, and promptly chose a garden salad.

'Guess what?' They were sitting over a cup of tea at the end of their lunch.

'What?' Tessa blinked.

'The ache in my shoulders is all gone.'

'Good. Perhaps I'll be able to hang out my shingle soon.'

'On the other hand, it could have something to do with our earlier...*talk.*' His smile strayed momentarily to the soft curve of her mouth. 'I got the distinct impression we'd lit a bit of a lamp somewhere, didn't you?'

Her heart gave a sideways skip. His meaning was quite clear. Was it possible? Dreamily, she let her fingers drift across to his and he took them, as if the action symbolised something—a future Tessa could only dream about.

CHAPTER SIX

BY FRIDAY Tessa realised her spirits had lifted almost without her noticing. Her grandmother's progress was slow but positive. Del had perked up considerably, even to the extent of being steady enough to get on with her knitting.

As for Tessa, she'd organised her days into blocks of work-time and sitting-with-Del time, only going home in the evenings when her grandmother had dropped off to sleep.

Now, this morning, as she hung out Del's laundry to dry in the fluttering breeze, she spared a thought for the people who had relatives and friends in hospital. It was certainly an extra stress but in her own case one she willingly accepted.

She loved her grandmother dearly.

In the kitchen, she hurriedly swallowed her coffee and half a piece of toast. She'd slept in and there'd been no one to chivvy her along. Alison was on days off and had gone home to her family at the Gold Coast.

To her relief, the night shift had been relatively quiet and Tessa was able to take the report without the added pressure of endless queries and follow-ups.

With duties allotted, she did a quick tour, meeting up with their first walking wounded for the day, a middle-aged woman whose white galoshes, overall and cloth cap proclaimed her workplace as the local meatworks. She was holding her hand wrapped in a thick dressing against her chest. Tessa recognised the young woman accompanying her as the nurse from the factory. 'Hi, Diane.' Tessa went forward to greet them.

'Hi.' Diane Allen made a small face. 'Not a great way to start the day, is it? This is Carmel Walters. She's had a small accident in the boning room—nasty gash to the palm of her hand. It'll need stitching.'

'Right, Carmel.' Tessa placed a sympathetic arm around the patient's shoulders and ushered her straight inside to the examination room. 'I'll find a doctor and we'll get you seen to.'

First she assigned Roz to make Mrs Walters more comfortable and then went to find their resident. She tracked him down in the staffroom. He was sitting at the table, his eyes closed, his hands cradling a mug of coffee. At Tessa's approach, he looked up and blinked.

'Suturing job for you in cube one, please, Brad.'

'Certainly, Sister.' He rocked to his feet.

'Are you sure you're OK to do it?' Tessa frowned. Was he even safe? Brad looked out on his feet.

'Yep, yep.' The resident nodded earnestly. 'Just wash my face.'

'When do you come off?'

His face creased into a tired grin. 'Tonight, if they can get cover.' He pushed his way into the bathroom. 'Be with you in a tick.'

Tessa shook her head. It was quite unacceptable, the long hours being worked by junior doctors in hospitals. No wonder there was burn-out all over the profession.

A trickle of emergencies kept her busy for the next little while and then, with the shift up and running, she decided she could safely take a few minutes out for her paperwork.

'I'll be in the office if I'm needed,' she told Carly.

'No worries.' The AIN's bright little face relaxed into an easy grin. 'I'll spread the word.'

Tessa fluttered her thanks, walking swiftly towards the sanctuary of Sister's office.

'Got a minute, Tessa?'

She whipped around, the sight of Luke putting a glitch in her heartbeat. Quickly diverting her eyes, she managed a suitably detached smile. 'Probably. Come on in.'

When they were seated, she looked at him expectantly.

'I've got John Abbott's results back.'

'Only now?' A tiny frown creased her forehead. 'They don't usually take this long.'

He twitched a shoulder. 'The tests I ordered were quite comprehensive.'

'So what are we looking at? Was it the thyroid, as you suspected?'

Luke nodded. 'Plus his iron stores are abysmally low. But his case isn't insurmountable. Unfortunately, after the tests, John insisted on discharging himself. The upshot is we'll need to get him back in here for a chat and started on some treatment. But it's not going to be straightforward, is it?'

'No.'

Luke tugged thoughtfully at his bottom lip. 'I'm

probably going to have to go and dig him out. Where did he say he was living?'

'At the back of Wheatley's garage.' Tessa sent him a dry look. 'Why do I get the feeling you're softening me up to go with you?'

He curved her a brief smile. 'Well, since you know him and he trusts you...'

'OK.' Tessa held up her hands in compliance. 'But if we could make it straight after my shift, please? I want to get back and visit Del, otherwise she'll have turned in. She's off to sleep rather early these days.'

'Shouldn't be a problem.' Luke got to his feet, seemingly satisfied with his bargain. 'Barring emergencies, of course, when we'd both be needed in any case.'

It was the first time Tessa had been in Luke's car.

'Wheatley's is only a few minutes away,' she said reprovingly. 'We could've walked.'

'You don't like my car?' He sounded offended.

She sank back in the soft leather seat, her eyes going to the discreet panelling that surrounded the latest in electronic gadgetry. 'It's very nice.'

'Anyway, there's method in my seeming slothfulness.' Luke came to the end of Cressbrook's main street and turned in the direction of the highway. 'I'm hoping we might be able to persuade John to come back to the hospital with us.'

Tessa looked thoughtful. 'Will you start him on thyroxine?'

'Mmm. But I'll need to monitor him to get the dose right. I've already had a phone consult with Mitchell Jarvis. An endocrinologist at Greenslopes hospital in Brisbane. He's of the opinion that once we can get John stable he won't look back. Providing he stays on his medication, of course.'

Tessa sent him a straight look. 'Strictly speaking, though, it's probably not a matter for A and E at all, is it?'

Luke's eyes narrowed momentarily. 'Don't start preaching budget constraints, Tessa. I could've stuck to the fine print and shunted him sideways to one of the GPs for follow-up, but do you see him keeping the appointment?'

Of course John wouldn't have. It obviously said something for Luke's persuasive powers in the first place that the young man had agreed to stay in hospital for the tests at all. 'We'll need to stop on the right, just past that stand of bamboo we're coming to,' she directed, and Luke slowed and brought his car to a smooth halt opposite the garage.

He switched off the engine. Late afternoon shadows had already crept over the landscape and they sat in a gentle pool of silence. There was wry amusement in Luke's blue eyes as he took in the outside of the typical country garage.

As well as its petrol pump and shelves of oil products on display, there was a splash of colour from the buckets of yellow and bronze chrysanthemums and beside them a tub of watermelons with a cardboard sign that proclaimed they were locally grown and two dollars each.

'The place is jumping, isn't it?' Luke drawled.

Bristling slightly at his inferred criticism, Tessa shrugged off her seat belt. 'Things just move a bit slower in the bush. But they get done just the same.'

'I'm sure.' Luke released the locks and they swung out of the car.

As they crossed the road, Tessa indicated a lane that ran beside the wooden garage building. 'The shed is at the end of this little easement. Let's just hope John's at home.'

Picking their way carefully, they climbed up the three rickety stairs, stepping beneath a fringe of trailing vine to the landing. Raising his hand, Luke knocked and called out but there was no answer and no sound from within.

He placed his hand on the doorknob. 'Shall we?'

Tessa rubbed her hands up and down her arms. She felt spooked suddenly. 'Can't do any harm, I suppose. And he could be ill,' she said as an afterthought, 'and not able to answer the door.'

'Only one way to find out.' The door showed a cantankerous resistance. In a second attempt, Luke shoved his knee against it to gain some extra leverage and finally it shuddered open and they stepped into the cool interior. Light came in from a fixed glass panel at the rear of the building.

They stood there in complete silence, until Tessa breathed, 'Oh, my goodness…' She shook her head, not believing what her eyes were telling her. The place was filled with artwork, unframed pictures of varying sizes and subjects, ranging from the simplicity of a dried flowerhead in a glass jar to the dramatic wildness of a summer storm.

'Hells bells…' Luke was clearly astonished. 'Are we to assume this is John's work?'

'I can see now where all his pension money goes,'

Tessa said quietly. 'He'd obviously rather paint than eat.'

'But he's improvised quite amazingly.' Luke pointed to where John had been mixing paints to great effect on a battered enamel plate. He'd also lined up a stack of cardboard cylinders from rolls of paper towels, which he was currently using as holders for his brushes.

'He's so talented, Luke, look at this!' Tessa pointed to a painting depicting everyday items on a cloth. 'They're so real I could reach out and pick them up. We absolutely must arrange a showing for him—'

'Steady on, Tess.' Luke urged caution. 'This isn't the time to be thinking of showings. In fact, I think we should get out of here. We're trespassing on very private space.' He rubbed a hand across his jaw. 'Let's ask at the garage, shall we? Maybe they've seen John about. But, then, on the other hand, I suppose he could be anywhere.'

Tessa made a small face. 'We could try his usual haunts—the Salvation Army for starters.'

John was nowhere to be found. Their initial enquiry at the garage provided no clue. 'He comes and goes.' Fred Wheatley shrugged. 'I don't keep tabs on him. Why would I?'

'He could show a bit of human interest,' Tessa fumed, as they settled back into Luke's car.

'Not everyone has your zeal for the underdog, Tess.' Luke pointed out evenly. 'And to his credit, Mr Wheatley does let John have the shed rent-free.'

'Big deal!'

The major at the Salvation Army house was more

helpful. 'John was here a couple of nights ago. Had a meal with us. Not that he ever eats much—skinny as a rake, that lad.'

'I think I'll alert the police,' Luke said quietly, when the remainder of Tessa's leads came to nothing.

'He'll hate that…'

'This is no time to be picky, Tessa.' Luke was firm. 'The man needs treatment urgently.'

'I know.' She shrugged dispiritedly. 'It just seems as though we're rounding him up like—like a stray dog or something.'

Luke let the silence hang between them. Tessa O'Malley's heart was almost bigger than she was, but there was a time when sympathy had to turn into substance. John Abbott's welfare was at stake and it was time to act. He changed down a gear to turn into the hospital car park. 'What are you going to do now?'

In an end-of-the-day gesture, Tessa raised her arms and stretched, dragging her fingers through her hair and shaking it out. 'Nip home to shower and change as a priority. Then I'll come back and sit with Del for a while. Why do you ask?'

He brought the car to a stop and switched off the engine. 'Since you'll be at the hospital anyway, I could knock us up something for dinner, if you like.'

Tessa looked up warily. 'At the doctors' residence?'

He lifted a shoulder. 'That's where I call home at the moment.'

'I don't know…' She looked across at him and her breath caught in her throat. Those flinty blue eyes were far too knowing. And suddenly she was afraid. Afraid of what seemed to be happening, whether she wanted it or not.

'I've invited you for a meal, Tessa.' His words fell just short of mocking her. 'Nothing else. Stop looking so threatened.'

'I'm not!' she said defensively. Jerkily, she leaned forward to gather up her shoulder-bag from the floor, scrunching it into a heap on her lap. She caught the inside of her bottom lip. 'I, um, just have one question.'

'Ask away.' He half smiled, as though humouring her.

'Can you cook or do I have take-away to look forward to?'

He sent her a pained look. 'Of course I can cook.'

Tessa tried on the three-quarter pants and promptly dragged them off in disgust. She spent her working hours wearing trousers—surely her leisure time deserved something a bit more dressy.

Her fingers riffled through the possibilities, finally coming up with a new addition to her summer wardrobe—a silk jersey dress of the latest geometrical print design, with tiny sleeves and a skirt that swung gracefully to her knees. She slipped it on, brushing her hair away from the wide neckline. Much better, she decided, peering in the mirror to fasten her gold loop earrings.

Picking up her car keys, she stepped out into the cool of early evening, aware her heart was racing. And as she reversed her Jeep out of the driveway and pointed it towards the hospital, she reminded herself that Luke had merely asked her to share a meal.

And tell that to the fairies! She gave a huff of self-admonishment. If the electric currents that had begun running between them from day one were anything to go by, food would be the last thing on their minds…

At the doctors' residence, the lights were blazing and Tessa could see Luke sitting on the front steps, knees drawn up, waiting for her. She blew out a calming breath and brought the Jeep to a halt, switching off the engine.

What would this evening bring? On a soft breath of apprehension, she pocketed her keys and slid out of the four-wheel-drive.

'Hello,' she greeted Luke softly, making her way up towards him, gripped by a blinding pleasure merely at seeing him there.

Luke pulled himself slowly upright. 'I didn't want to start dinner too early in case you wanted a little extra time with Del.'

'She sent me off.' Standing beside him, Tessa beat off a sense of shyness. 'Wanted to look at her usual Friday programme on TV.'

'Well, that's a good sign.' Luke began ushering her inside. 'Shows she's getting back her interest in life.'

'Yes, I suppose so. It's very quiet,' she deflected quickly. 'Do we have the place to ourselves?'

'For the moment.' His tone was dry. 'Don't bet on it lasting. You've been here before, I take it?'

'Now and again for the odd party.' She followed

him into the kitchen. 'Can I do anything to help with dinner?'

He sent her a smile that curled her toes. 'You could pour us a glass of wine. There's some red opened and breathing on the counter.'

Tessa found glasses and poured the wine and then watched as he expertly tossed onions, tomatoes and herbs in a pan. She picked up her glass, lacing both hands around it. 'You really do know your way around the kitchen.'

'Surprised?' He glanced up from sprinkling Parmesan on the pasta, moving her out of the way to get to a drawer behind her. 'My brother's a chef. You should see me whip up a lemon sorbet with coconut praline.'

'You're making it up.' She laughed, taking his glass of wine and handing it across to him.

'Would I lie?' He grinned, touching her glass with his.

'So, where does your brother work?' Tessa made herself comfortable on one of the high-backed kitchen stools.

'At the Sheraton in Brisbane.' Luke turned back to the stove to give his ingredients in the pan a final stir. 'He's recently married. In fact, he was married on the Saturday I arrived here in Cressbrook.'

So that's why he'd been travelling so late at night. 'You'd been at the wedding?'

'Mmm. I was Andre's best man.'

'And who was the bride?'

'Nina Blaine.' He scooped the tomato mixture from the pan and folded it into the pasta. 'She has a fashion salon in the Wintergarden Mall in Brisbane.'

'Nina's?' Tessa sent him a quizzical look. 'I know the salon. Some of us used to go there to see the latest trends when I was working at St Anne's. Can't say I ever bought anything, though.'

Luke set the plates down on the long refectory table. 'It's pretty exclusive. Her stuff costs an arm and a leg, from what I hear.'

'Ah!' Tessa's eyes gleamed with speculation. 'She has money, then?'

'Her old man does.' Luke held the chair out and Tessa took her place at the table.

'Does yours?' she asked cheekily.

His expression became shuttered. 'Not any more.' The words hung in the air for a second until he forced out a crooked smile. 'Now, Miss O'Malley, let's eat before the food gets cold and all my efforts to impress you will have been in vain.'

The meal was delicious and she told him so.

He lifted a shoulder modestly. 'What about you? What's your culinary forte?'

An imp of mischief danced in Tessa's eyes. 'Cakes.'

'Cakes!' Luke chuckled, pretending to cast a discerning look at her figure. 'I'd never have guessed.'

She showed him the tip of her tongue. 'I make them, Doctor. I didn't say I ate them.'

Luke's laugh was rich and deep. Hell, it felt good to have her here. Better than good. His eyes caressed her over the rim of his glass. Every time he looked at her he came alive inside, wanting her.

He took a sip of his wine, blade-sharp desire hitting him out of nowhere, bringing with it a replay of the way they'd been together on that Sunday on the grassy bank of the creek, when their hands and mouths had said so much more than words ever could…

Even now, as he looked at her, he ached to touch her intimately, to stroke the smoothness of her skin, to kiss the tiny hollow at the base of her throat, breathe in the sweet scent of her tangled hair.

He drew in a deep breath, a wave of reaction causing him to seek a more comfortable position in his chair as he clenched his fingers around the stem of his wineglass. They needed time to sort out exactly what they wanted from each other. And time was something they didn't have. Or not enough of it anyway.

Unless he rushed her. His mouth drew into a thin line. That was something he'd vowed he wouldn't do.

Later, as they packed the dishwasher, Tessa couldn't believe the evening had gone so fast. They'd sat talking over several cups of coffee. Although they'd swapped opinions about many topics, she realised that so much more was being left unsaid.

And that idea was strangely unsettling.

'Did you have any luck getting on to the police about John?'

'Sorry?'

Tessa repeated the question, flicking him a startled glance. He was eyeing her thoughtfully and his gaze had gone all smoky…

'Yes, I did.' Luke brought himself together with a snap. 'They'll let me know when they locate him. The sergeant thought it may be as soon as tonight.'

'You'll admit him again?'

'Mmm, I'd like to.' His brow creased. 'I'm betting on him feeling so much better after the thyroxine kicks in that he'll be ready to start making some changes to his lifestyle.'

'Like getting a permanent place to live.' Tessa placed their glasses carefully in the plastic basket inside the dishwasher. 'The Salvation Army would seem the best option for him in the interim. And at least they'll feed him. Then let's hope he can start making some practical use out of all this talent he's been given.'

A bark of laughter and a clatter of footsteps along the hallway had them both turning. Luke glanced at his watch and said ruefully, 'Looks like the troops are home.'

Tessa flipped the door closed on the dishwasher. 'It's time I was, too.'

'Hi, guys,' Brad and his counterpart, Gerard Gallagher, plonked their parcels of fish and chips and six-packs of beer on the table. 'Not disturbing you, are we?' Brad crinkled a grin at them. It was obvious he'd had a few drinks already.

'Not at all.' Tessa's smile was warm. Poor guy, he deserved a bit of space to unwind. 'Finally got some time off, have you, Brad?'

'Day and a half.' He rubbed his hands together in obvious anticipation. 'But right now we're about to watch the footy. Come on, Jez.' He prodded his contemporary. 'Let's get in front of the telly.'

'Who's your money on?' Luke's gaze sparked with interest.

'The eels. Who else?' The two young men gathered up their food and turned in the direction of the recreation room.

'We're Sydney lads, mate.' Gerard tossed a cocky grin back at Luke. 'We'll beat the hell out of your Brisbane pack, no worries. Watch the game with us?' He angled his head towards the sound of the television.

'Maybe later,' Luke said with a grin. He shook his head. 'Was I ever that young?'

'Feeling your age, Grandpa?' Tessa stifled a giggle. And quite without thinking, and because it seemed the most natural reaction in the world, she turned and slipped her hands into his, tightening her fingers and feeling him respond. 'Come and see me off—if you can manage the steps?'

'Cheeky monkey.' His lips brushed softly against her hair before he wrapped her closely to his side.

Moonlight bathed the forecourt in soft luminosity and a flurry of tropical wind stirred the leaves into whispers as they made their way slowly down the front stairs and across the asphalt to her Jeep.

'You're OK to drive, aren't you?'

'Of course.' A little awkwardly, Tessa fished the keys from her pocket and bent to insert them into the lock. She gave a throaty laugh, tipping her head back to look at him. 'I only had one glass of wine and I've probably drowned that with all those cups of coffee.'

'I wish you didn't have to go,' he murmured softly.

His meaning was clear and she felt a fluttering inside, her mind zeroing in on the fact that Alison was away and tonight her house was empty…

'I want to be with you, Tess…' His hands stroked up her arms before he gathered her in, tightening his arms around her so that she felt the imprint of him from thigh to breast.

'Luke…' She gusted a small indrawn breath, feeling his hands on her lower back, tilting her closer still, and the sweet sting of anticipation slithered up her spine.

'Just say the word,' he said indistinctly against the side of her throat.

Could she? Dared she? Winding her arms around his neck, she closed her eyes, picturing him as her lover, dreaming of his body claiming hers so completely, so fully. So honestly.

When he took her mouth, the feeling of oneness was so piercing, so intense, so tangible that she almost gave the answer he wanted to hear. But a little voice in her head kept insisting that nothing was that simple. Nothing.

'Luke, let me go.' She wrenched back, unable to hide the panic in her voice. But as she tried to draw her arms away he gripped them tighter, and the slightest tug of war began.

'Stop fighting me!' Luke contained her, holding her very still for a moment, and then he let her go. His eyes glittered. 'For crying out loud, Tessa, did you imagine I was about to force myself on you?'

For a second Tessa was frozen, immobilised with shock. 'I think I'd better go,' she said unsteadily. He'd ruined the evening and capped it all by making her feel foolish and pathetic. 'Could you stand aside, please?'

'Come on, Tess, don't be like that. Come here…'

He opened his arms but she hesitated. Too long. 'What's this all about?' His frown deepened. 'Has someone tried to—?'

'No!' She backed away, her arms wrapping across her midriff. 'No, of course not. You frightened me a little, that's all.'

'That's all!' Luke scoffed a laugh, spearing his hands viciously through his hair. 'Your reaction was completely over the top.'

'This is getting us nowhere.' Tessa was appalled to hear a catch in her voice. 'You're obviously working to your own agenda, Luke. You don't miss an opportunity to start coming on to me—'

'And you're the passive recipient, are you, Tessa?' His face was like granite and his voice was deathly quiet. 'Pardon me if I don't quite believe that.'

'Go to hell!' She dragged the door of the Jeep half-open and stood there, her head tossed back, glaring at him.

'What are you going to do now?' he said heavily, his feet planted firmly apart and his arms folded across his chest. 'Run over me?'

'Don't tempt me!'

'But you know I do,' he mocked laconically. 'All the time.'

Then, very deliberately, he leaned across her to pull the door of the Jeep right open. 'Sleep on that, Tess—if you can.'

All the strength had drained from Tessa's legs like water from spaghetti, and her knees were shaking so much she could hardly stand. But she managed to, knowing she couldn't leave things like this. With so much strain between them, the tension would begin to spill over into the other areas of her life. And her job would become untenable.

'We have to work together, Luke.' She forced the words past the dryness in her throat. 'I don't want to fight with you.'

'Then don't.' He gave a ragged sigh. 'God knows, it's the last thing I want. Do you have a shift tomorrow?'

As if all her muscle supports had suddenly let go, Tessa dropped into the driver's seat and swung her legs in. 'I have a late.'

'I'll probably see you about the place, then.' The backs of his fingers brushed against her hair as he released the seat belt and settled it across her shoulder. 'I'm on call.'

CHAPTER SEVEN

LISTENING to Tessa drive away, discerning the rapid change of gears as she climbed to third, Luke tried to untangle the strands of emotion inside him.

Making his way slowly back up the stairs, he owned to frustration and anger, and the oddest kind of pain he couldn't account for. It was as though it was all centred around his heart and squeezing the life from it.

And watching a football match on television with a couple of exuberant residents was about as appealing as diagnosing a patient with piles. Dark humour edged his mouth and he went into his bedroom. Ignoring the house rules, he flung himself down on the counterpane, boots and all, and stared at the ceiling.

Tessa O'Malley.

She'd got to him, as no other woman had in his thirty-four years. He was entranced by everything about her. God, her physicality for a start. And her spirit, her sassiness, her incredible *heart*. Which was probably another way of saying her strength of character, he supposed.

He snorted a soft laugh. When before had he ever brought that last attribute into the male-female equation? So why now did it matter so much that Tessa thought well of *him*? Because it did. A whole lot.

* * *

Tessa went on duty next day at three, hoping some hard physical work would help to ease the yearning, unsettling ache deep inside her. Add to that the queasy feeling in her stomach and you just about had it right, she thought distractedly, locking her Jeep and making her way across the car park to the A and E entrance.

She hadn't slept properly. But, then, why on earth had she expected to after what had happened between her and Luke?

I wish he'd never come here! At least repeating the mantra helped rekindle her own anger so that it throbbed inside her as painfully as her hurt and disillusionment.

But when she tried to analyse her anger, she didn't get very far. Why was she even directing her anger at Luke? Shouldn't it be at herself for not going after what her heart was telling her she wanted, needed?

And she'd given him so many mixed signals last night. Had done since they'd met if she was truthful. Oh, lord. She rolled her bottom lip between her teeth. No wonder he'd hit out at her with those snide comments…

Sighing, she put her bag in her locker and went to take the report, only to find they were short-staffed yet again. And Gwyneth was rostered on her shift.

Barely thirty minutes later, the atmosphere was fraut and she was asking urgently, 'Has anyone seen Luke?'

'He was here earlier,' said Wendy Green, one of the mature assistants in nursing who worked only on the weekends. 'Better bleep him, Tess. He may have gone back to the residence.'

'Hi.' Luke strode up to the nurses' station within moments of her bleeping him.

'Hi.' Tessa forced a travesty of a smile through stiff lips.

His brow creased into a frown. 'What's up?'

She took a deep breath and launched into speech. 'We've had an emergency call relayed from the ambulance base. A farmer, Alan Fielding, is being brought in by his wife. Severe neck wound.'

Luke grimaced. 'What happened? Do we know?'

'He was out mustering, rode his motorbike into a single-strand wire fence. Profuse bleeding to the right side of his neck.'

'Can we expect arterial damage?'

'The base didn't know for sure. He managed to hold the wound together with his fingers and somehow stumbled the five hundred metres to the house. His wife didn't want to hang about waiting for the ambulance. She made a snap decision to bring him in herself. I've alerted Theatre.'

'What's the ETA?'

'They're only three k's out of town so they'll be here directly.'

'Right.' Luke was tight-lipped. 'Get someone to wait with a wheelchair at the entrance and we'd better run a check on what we'll need in Resus.' His eyes flicked over her. 'You sure you're OK with this?'

Did he mean was she OK about working with him? Tessa fought for composure. The look he'd given her had been only fleeting but long enough for her to see his eyes were red-rimmed. Obviously, he hadn't slept any better than she had.

But there was no time for that distraction now. They could well have a life-and-death situation on their hands. She sent him a very straight look. 'I'm fine.'

'Mrs Fielding sounds a resourceful lady.' Luke was immediately all business as they prepared Resus. 'Let's just hope she's kept our patient sitting up.'

They didn't have long to wait to find out. There was the unmistakable crunching sound of a wheelchair arriving and suddenly the resus doors were flung open.

'I didn't let him lie down on account of the bleeding.' Cheryl Fielding cast a frantic look at the faces in the room.

'You did very well, Mrs Fielding.' Luke took a share of the weight, and with the wardsman's help the injured man was transferred to the treatment couch.

'Steady!' Luke cautioned. 'Keep him upright!'

'Please, will he be all right?'

'The doctor will look after your husband now and you'll be able to see him before he goes to Theatre.' Wendy Green was there, calmly removing Cheryl from the scene. 'We'll need to get some details from you, and I'm sure you could do with a cup of tea...'

Alan was groggy but conscious.

'G'day, Doc...' he slurred.

'Save your strength, Alan,' Luke said gently. 'We'll do the very best we can for you.' He whipped out his stethoscope. 'Right, let's see what we're dealing with here.' He listened intently, checking the man's breathing. 'Seems OK.'

He tossed the stethoscope aside and very carefully

removed the thick bath towel from around Alan's throat, examining the wound swiftly but with clinical thoroughness.

'Main aorta is intact. You've been lucky, mate. Clamps, please, Tessa.'

She handed him the instrument resembling a cross between a pair of scissors and a pair of pliers, and systematically he began a temporary closure of the wound. 'Would you dress it now, please?'

Tessa was ready with several thick pads to staunch any residual bleeding. 'He's ready for oxygen.' She looked sharply at Luke. 'What capacity do you want it?'

He made a moue of his bottom lip. 'Make it eight litres a minute. And get an oximeter on him, please. We'll see what that tells us.'

Tessa worked automatically, dovetailing with Luke as they carried out the emergency procedures swiftly. The probe was in place on the injured man's finger, allowing them to monitor the amount of oxygen saturation in his blood.

'There's no time to wait for a cross-match. That'll have to come later.' Luke was already preparing an IV line. 'We'll run haemacell in the interim. Could you check the wound again for any bleeding, please?'

'Some seepage but it's holding.' Tessa replaced the loose dressing. Taking a reading from the oximeter, she reported to Luke, 'Oxygen sats ninety per cent.'

'Got a BP reading?' Luke began scribbling on Alan's chart.

'One hundred over sixty. Pulse one-twenty. Respiration twenty-four. What drugs do you need?'

'Better make it fifty milligrams of pethidine and ten of Maxolon. His tummy's got to be in turmoil after this lot.'

'I'll get the drugs.' Tessa was already at the door.

When she returned with the painkiller and anti-emetic, she could see Luke wasn't taking any chances.

Their patient had been placed on a heart monitor. The three sticky dots over the chest area were attached to a little box like a clock radio that would keep them apprised of his heart rate. If the injured farmer should suddenly begin to bleed out, the medical team would be alerted immediately.

'Thanks.' Luke looked fleetingly at Tessa before he took the prepared drugs and sent the injection home. 'I'll have a word with Mrs Fielding and then I'll scrub.' He passed a hand across his face to massage his temples. 'I know the shift is short-staffed but I'd be grateful if you'd monitor Alan yourself.'

'Certainly.'

'And escort him to Theatre?'

'Yes, Doctor, of course,' she acknowledged in her polite, professional voice.

It was nine o'clock before Tessa saw Luke again. Her heart bounced sickeningly when he appeared at the nurses' station.

Automatically, she turned aside from her paperwork to greet him. He looked like hell. What did that mean? Her stomach plummeted and she searched his face for clues about the condition of Alan Fielding, but there was only a taut preoccupation in his expression. She quickly swallowed the ache in her throat. 'How did it go?'

He gave an open-handed shrug. 'Pretty well. I could've done with an extra pair of hands, though. Mrs Fielding about?' He swung his head to look back towards Reception. 'I couldn't find her in the lounge.'

'She's still here in Casualty, actually.' Tessa came from behind the counter. 'Wendy took her under her wing and she asked if she could stay. Is there a problem?'

'No. But I need to put her in the picture before she sees her husband.' His hand drummed on the counter-top for a second. 'Could you bring her along to my office, perhaps?' The corners of his mouth compressed ruefully. 'Any chance of a coffee in the meantime?'

'Every chance, I should think.' Tessa flicked him a guarded smile. 'And a couple of paracetamol to go with it?' She'd seen the papery look around his eyes and diagnosed a king-sized headache.

'How did you guess?' His hand reached out towards her cheek, then drew sharply back before it could connect with her skin.

'Put it down to my powers of observation.' She hadn't missed the aborted caress and something inside her died a little more at the way things between them had become so muddled. So muddled that every spontaneous gesture was now liable to be misinterpreted, every nuance suspect.

* * *

'Sister, would you mind staying, please?' In his office, Luke proffered chairs for Tessa and Mrs Fielding and then resumed his own seat.

'Everyone's been so kind.' Cheryl Fielding's hands were clasped tightly on her lap. 'Nurse Wendy even found me a clean top.' She bit her lips together. 'Mine was all over blood—how is he, Doctor?' She tacked the query on quickly, as though she couldn't wait a second longer to find out what was happening with her husband.

Luke spread his hands on the desktop in front of him. 'The surgery went well, Mrs Fielding, but there are some things you need to know.' He met Cheryl's gaze calmly, before continuing, 'Don't be alarmed when you see Alan. Because of his injuries, he'll have to be nursed sitting upright in bed.'

Cheryl's eyes widened momentarily in apprehension, before she said quietly, 'I understand, Doctor. Will he know me?'

'Of course, but he won't be able to speak for possibly the next couple of days.'

'Oh...' Cheryl's hand went sharply to her throat. 'I never thought— What will he look like? I mean, will he have tubes and things?'

Tessa noted the narrowing of Luke's eyes and the tiny inclination of his head, and sensed it was time for her to come in. 'Your husband will have an IV line in, Cheryl. Part of its function will be to run medication into his system for pain relief. And he'll have a nose tube as well. We can't take a chance on him vomiting. As you can imagine, that kind of exertion would be very painful for him with the wound to his throat so new.' Not to say downright dangerous, she tacked on silently.

Cheryl looked stunned, her gaze going from Tessa to Luke and back again. 'He's not going to die, is he?'

'No, he isn't, Cheryl.' Tessa leaned across and gave the woman's shoulder a comforting little squeeze.

'He's never been in hospital…' Cheryl beat back tears with the heels of her hands. 'We've only been here a few months. Alan took an early retirement package from his firm—he's only fifty-five. And we bought the farm. Now I'm wondering if we did the right thing. Sorry—I didn't mean to go on like this…'

'You're just reacting to the shock of it all,' Tessa came in kindly. 'But, honestly, once Alan is over the hump of the first few days, things will start looking much brighter.'

'Sister's right,' Luke said gently. 'Alan's recovery may seem a bit slow initially, but when he's up to taking his food again things will seem much more positive.'

'When will that be, Doctor?' Cheryl asked shakily. 'When he can starting eating again, I mean?'

'We'll have a speech therapist review his swallow in a few days' time. And if there's no problem and we're happy with the rest of his progress, he'll be able to start on a puréed diet. We'll upgrade that as he tolerates it.'

'I see.' Cheryl began to dab her eyes with the tissues Tessa had unobtrusively provided. 'It all makes perfect sense now you've explained it. Thank you both so much.' She favoured them with a watery smile. 'Can I see my husband now?'

Tessa got to her feet. 'I'll take you up.'

'Where the hell are we going to find a speech therapist?'

Tessa had come back from the surgical ward to find Luke firmly entrenched in Sister's office, writing up his notes.

'Sorry?' her brows knitted in sudden irritation. It had been a long twenty-four hours and she'd been awake for most of them. As a result, her eyes had begun to feel gritty and her feet hurt. And despite all their preparation, Cheryl had fallen to pieces when she'd seen her husband and Tessa had just finished mopping her up and settling her down again.

'A speech therapist,' he repeated mildly. 'I don't imagine they're too thick on the ground in Cressbrook.'

'Why would you think that?' Tessa perceived an arrogance in his comment and took it to heart. Just like that, he'd again prejudged rural medicine and found it wanting.

She simmered through the beat of silence and then Luke looked up. He raised an eyebrow. 'I've said the wrong thing, haven't I?'

Give the man a prize, Tessa muttered inwardly. 'We share a speech therapist with the education department. Romy Glasson is her name. She works part time at the school and does stuff for us when we need her.'

'That sounds like a sensible arrangement.' Luke slid his ballpoint pen back into his pocket. 'So, I can count on Surgical to liaise with her when we're ready for Alan's assessment, is that so?'

'Yes.' Tessa rescued the computer from the screen-saver and touched a few keys. 'It's usually Benita.'

'I'll make a mental note of that.'

'Good.' Tessa couldn't help herself. She lifted her chin and turned her head, searing her gaze with his. And suddenly it was all happening again, the need she felt around him to be held, comforted.

Loved.

'I'm overdue for a break.' She looked away, jumping into speech too brightly. 'Can I interest you in some home-made soup?'

'Sounds good.' In the complexity of the silence that followed, Luke didn't stop to analyse his thoughts. It seemed safer not to. Instead, he followed his heart, getting slowly to his feet and moving around the desk towards her until he was close enough to tilt her chin with the tips of his middle and index fingers.

'I don't want us to lose each other, Tess.' He looked at her through half-closed eyes. 'If only you would…'

'Would what?' Her breath caught and she found herself shaking, powerless beneath that moody blue appraisal.

'Trust me a little.'

Her eyes widened. 'I do trust you, Luke.' And like a bolt of lightning, the thought struck. She did trust him. Absolutely.

'You do?' He drew back, as if the declaration had momentarily startled him.

Tessa shook her head impatiently. 'It's the situation we find ourselves in I distrust. You're here today and gone to the other side of the world tomorrow.'

'Not quite tomorrow.' His mouth compressed. 'You're saying the timing's all wrong, is that it?'

'Something like that.' She stayed stiff.

'And a lot more.' A soft oath left his mouth. 'You've been burned, haven't you?' The painful, frozen look on her face goaded him into a harsh resolve. 'Who was he? I'll break his bloody neck!'

Tessa swallowed a half-smile. 'You'll have to go to England for that. And it's ancient history anyway.'

'Who was he?' Luke repeated thinly.

'A locum SR at St Anne's,' she said crossly. 'And how did we get into this in the first place?'

'Because you looked a bit lost, Tess. And sad…' Without thinking, he reached out and his arms went round her.

It turned into a hug and nothing more. As if suddenly realising where they were, they pulled back almost as one but not before Tessa had registered that her nerve-endings were tingling and her breathing felt uncomfortably tight.

'I don't still have feelings for him, if that's what you're thinking.' She lifted her head, refusing to flinch. 'It just galls me sometimes to think I gave so much to the relationship and it was all built on sand. Only I didn't know it at the time.' She shoved the chair in, turning away so he couldn't see her expression.

'I'm not him, Tess.'

The words were careful, guarded in the extreme, but they lingered like the last rays of sunset over the horizon. 'I hear what you're saying, Luke,' she said quietly.

Somehow they got to the staffroom.

'What can I do to help?' Luke asked.

'Nothing.' Tessa waved him to a chair. 'I've only to microwave the soup and make a bit of toast—that's if there's any bread left.' She checked the container. 'Praise be. One slice or two?'

'Ah...' He looked a bit sheepish. 'I could manage three, if there's enough.'

Tessa chuckled, snuggling like a kitten into the bubble of happiness that surrounded her.

There was a sheen of softness in Luke's eyes as he watched her neat, co-ordinated movements. In under five minutes she'd set a bowl of piping hot vegetable soup and several rounds of toast in front of him.

'Butter or margarine? There's both.' Tessa bent and got the tubs from the fridge.

Luke began to spread his toast. 'I must say there's always lashings of food in this place. Very different from most hospitals I've worked in. How come?'

Tessa took up her spoon. 'It's down to the Women's Auxiliary mainly. They have fundraisers all the time for the hospital. Our nursing supervisor receives a lump sum at the beginning of each month and it's her brief to make sure the staff kitchens are well stocked. Often we don't get time to eat when other people normally do.'

'My stomach tells me that quite frequently,' Luke said drily.

'And the committee haven't stopped there. Over

time, they've gone through each department, systematically upgrading our electrical appliances.'

Luke shook his head. 'That's amazing. Surely it must make you feel valued by the community?'

Tessa lifted a shoulder. 'It does, and on the whole staff morale is pretty good—except when we can't get senior doctors to come and work here.' She lifted her lashes on a meaningful little look.

His brows shot up. '*I'm* here, aren't I?'

'And obviously you didn't have to be dragged here, kicking and screaming, like most of them,' she conceded with a laugh.

If only she knew how he'd fought tooth and nail *not* to come. Luke passed her the toast. Should he tell her the real reason he was here in Cressbrook? Because he wouldn't have been able to access his funding to America otherwise?

It seemed dishonest to let her go on thinking he'd been struck with a burst of public-spiritedness towards rural health. But would it lessen her trust in him if she knew? He couldn't take the chance. Not yet.

'No sign of John Abbott?' Tessa pushed her empty bowl away. 'There was nothing on the report.'

Luke shook his head. 'Let's hope we're not looking for a body.'

Her head flew up and she looked at him in horror. 'You don't think—?'

'No. Not really, I suppose.' Luke scrubbed a hand across his jaw. 'It's more likely he's found a new hidey-hole. He'll no doubt come out when he's ready. In any event, I've alerted the appropriate people here so that, if we're not on duty, John will be seen and treated without delay.'

'I hope so.'

'Hope he'll be treated?' Without warning, his hand reached out and covered hers.

'No. I meant, I hope John turns up soon…' Tessa stared down at the hand covering hers.

Their eyes met and suddenly the atmosphere was emotionally charged again.

'You…and I, Tess…' Slowly, Luke began to separate her fingers with his thumb, touching the tip of each one as he moved across her hand. 'We have to talk properly, don't we?'

She nodded, unable to speak. Every nerve in her body tightened, became electrified with sensation. She swallowed thickly. 'Are you off tomorrow?'

'Mmm.' Abruptly, he pulled away, leaning back in his chair. He ran a hand through his hair with obvious frustration. 'But I have to make a quick trip to Brisbane. Some loose ends to tie up. Back late on Monday.'

Tessa was aware of holding herself very still. 'I start a week of night duty on Monday. I'm not very approachable without my proper sleep, I'm afraid. And somehow I'll have to keep up my visits to Del.'

She watched his eyes cloud. 'You're spreading yourself too thinly, Tess.'

'Rats! I've done it a zillion times. Anyway…' She shrugged. 'There's nothing I can do about it.' He watched her chin come up in that bright, elfin-like way he was coming to recognise. 'So I guess I'll see you when I see you, then.'

'That's not very satisfactory.' Luke's statement

was gruff. 'Perhaps, one evening, we could have dinner together, or something?'

'Perhaps…' She bit her lip, adding carefully, 'You could come to my house.'

A tiny pulse flickered in Luke's cheek. Was she saying what he thought she was saying? He gave a taut smile. 'You've mentioned a housemate…'

She gave the faintest nod. 'Alison James.'

'Then…' He frowned. 'Do I take it that it will be dinner for three?'

Tessa's gaze widened and then dropped abruptly to the table. 'She's on lates next week. It will be just the two of us…'

CHAPTER EIGHT

'THANK heavens you're still here, Dr Stretton!' Wendy came hurtling through the door. Her face was white with shock.

'What is it?' Luke and Tessa shot upright.

'MVA.' Wendy's hand went to her heart. 'It's Sue Mitchell.'

'Oh, my God!' Tessa turned frantic eyes to Luke. 'She's pregnant!'

'Take it easy.' Luke held up a calming hand. 'How far along is she?'

Tessa bit her lip. 'About ten weeks, I think.'

Luke frowned. The worse possible time in any pregnancy for something like this to happen—not that there was ever a good time to have a motor vehicle accident, he reflected grimly. 'What do we know, Wendy? Was anyone else involved? Her husband?'

The assistant in nursing shook her head. 'Sue was the sole occupant of her car, the base said. It was hit from behind. They should be here in five minutes.'

'Right.' Luke turned to Tessa. 'Would you make sure the Resus room is ready, please? And check there's a radiographer on hand. At some stage we'll need to do an ultrasound. I'll go and wait for the ambulance.'

Tessa began issuing orders swiftly. 'Gwyneth, would you phone the golf club and see if Iain

Mitchell is still at work, please? If he is, tell him we need him here. My guess is that Sue was on her way to collect him when the accident happened. The number's by the phone, and stay calm and professional, please.'

'Yes, Tessa. This is terrible. Poor Sue...' Gwyneth, for once shaken out of her usual uninvolved attitude, hurried away.

'Sue's waited years for this baby,' Wendy clamped her bottom lip between her teeth. 'She can't lose it. She can't!'

'She won't,' Tessa said bracingly. 'Not if we can help it.'

And Luke was here. Tessa clung to the thought for dear life.

All at once her nerves began to tauten as the growl of the ambulance siren sounded and then was abruptly cut when the vehicle reached the receiving bay.

Then it was everyone combining their skills to the limits as Sue was rushed into Resus.

'Tess...' She was shivering, her eyes wide in trepidation. 'Thank God it's you! My baby...'

'Hang in there, honey.' Tessa took Sue's hand and squeezed it. 'We're all here for you and Iain's on his way. Have you felt any bleeding?'

'N-no.' Sue took a shaky breath. 'And I would've known, wouldn't I?'

'You would.' Tessa projected calm, even though her insides were shaking. 'I'll just take a look.' A few moments later, she was able to report, 'So far, so good. But we'll pop a pad on so we can monitor you.'

'I don't want to lose this baby—'

'Sue,' Luke interposed gently, 'we'll do everything we can to stop that happening. Right now, I need to check your tummy for any injury from your seat belt.' He exchanged a tense look with Tessa. They both knew that if the seat belt had impacted forcibly, Sue could have a ruptured spleen.

As a nurse herself, Sue was only too well aware of the possibility. 'The impact from the other car wasn't all that bad.' She gave a ragged little breath. 'More of a nudge, really. But it was one of those big four-wheel-drives and I've only a little hatchback…'

Luke's hands worked their way methodically across her stomach, palpating, checking, rechecking. Finally, he lifted his head.

'You seem to have escaped any spleen damage, Sue. Now, let's just see what the rest of you is doing, shall we?' He turned to Tessa, his brows raised in silent query.

'BP and pulse slightly elevated but nowhere near what it would be if she was bleeding internally.'

Luke let out a relieved breath. Turning back to his patient, he flicked a torch in her eyes to check her pupils were normal and reacting. He gave an affirmative little nod. 'Uh-huh. OK, Sue, squeeze my hand. Good. Let's check your legs and feet now for any deficits. OK, that's fine.'

His dark head was bent close to Tessa's. 'I think she's stable enough for us to run a check on the baby. Could you pass me the Doppler, please?'

Tessa spread a film of gel on Sue's abdomen and then held her hand as Luke ran the special obstetric stethoscope over her slight bump. For a few moments his expression was grave and Tessa's heart plummeted. Then, miraculously, it lightened. 'Nice regular beat, Sue, but we'll do an ultrasound to make absolutely sure.'

'Oh, thank God.' Tears spilled from Sue's eyes and down her cheeks. 'I was so scared...'

'Iain's here.' Gwyneth popped her head around the door.

'Two minutes.' Luke flicked a hand backwards. 'I'd like to admit you overnight, Sue. We'll put you on a saline drip and I'd like to run a blood test as well, just to make sure your haemoglobin levels are where they should be.'

'Same old, same old.' Sue gave a weak laugh. 'Don't worry, I'll be the best patient ever.'

'Don't be surprised if you feel some muscle soreness by the morning.' Luke paused with his hand on the end of the treatment couch. 'There could be a bit of residual whiplash involved. I'll put you down for Nurofen as a precaution.'

'Thanks, Luke.' Sue's temporary composure began to crumple. 'Thank you so much. And you, Tess...'

Luke shook his head. 'Be a pretty poor show if we couldn't look after one of our own. I'll see your GP gets your notes.'

Tessa was halfway through her week's rota of night duty when she saw Luke again. He wandered into Sister's office about midnight.

'How have you been?' he asked softly.

'Fine.' She flushed, covering her confusion by gathering up her paperwork and tapping it into a neat pile. 'You?' She retrieved a stethoscope from the back of a chair, waved it about for a moment and then absently placed it in the out-tray.

'I'm fine, too.' Luke parked himself across the corner of the desk. 'What's the latest on Sue? Have you been in touch?'

'Yes. She and Iain are having a few days' holiday. He wants her to leave work and take it easy until the baby arrives.'

Luke raised a dark brow. 'Is that what Sue wants?'

'Not really. Financially, it's not practical for a start.'

His mouth turned down. 'Money, or rather, lack of it, can be a real pain.'

'I imagine they'll work something out.'

'The hospital can't afford to lose people of the calibre of Sue.'

Tessa lifted a shoulder. 'She may come back part time. But the reality is she earns more than Iain and it's all a bit difficult.'

'What does he do?'

Tessa made a small face. 'Bar attendant at the golf club. He has to work a fair bit of overtime to bring home a decent wage. According to Sue, he always wanted to do something with horticulture, even completed a year or so at college after he left high school. But then his father got sick and Iain had to come home and help out.' She shrugged. 'They lost the farm anyway so I imagine he must sometimes wonder if it was all worth it.'

'Perhaps he could re-train for something?'

Tessa laughed a bit off-key. 'Opportunity would be a fine thing.'

'It was just a thought.' Luke's gaze narrowed on her face. Almost without her noticing, he'd slid off the desk and stood, blocking her way, as she tried to get to the filing cabinet. In a deliberate movement he reached out and cupped her cheek, his thumb stroking along her cheekbone and down to her chin.

'W-what are you doing?' She swallowed, slowly allowing herself to look up to meet the vividly demanding question in his eyes.

'Dinner tomorrow night?'

She licked her lips. 'I suppose…yes.'

'Sure?'

She nodded and murmured, 'Do you have my address?' No, of course he didn't. 'I live in Cyclamen Avenue.'

A smile flickered around his mouth. 'Sounds very grand.'

'Doesn't it just?' She stifled a giggle.

'Sevenish?'

'Or earlier…' Her voice caught and her gaze flickered all the way down his body and back up again.

He dipped his head to hide a smile. 'I'll see what I can do.'

Tessa came off duty at seven the following morning. Her skin prickled as she thought of Luke's nocturnal visit. Perhaps she'd dreamt it? She bit back a spurt of laughter. She hadn't dreamt it. The touch of his fingers on her skin had been too real for that. Accelerating her Jeep out of the hospital car park, she headed for home.

Had she thought things through enough? she fretted, her fingers unsteady as she opened the front door. Yet the moment she entered the quiet, welcoming space of her home, she felt an absolute rightness with her decision to invite Luke here.

Excitement was giving her an artificial wakefulness. Showered and dressed in a pair of loose pyjamas, she made breakfast and took it outside to the pergola in the back garden. A wistful smile curved her mouth. Whatever the season, the old wooden structure was one of her favourite places to linger, she decided, looking to where the weathered timbers held up the trailing vines of wisteria and jasmine.

She ate a leisurely breakfast of muesli, fruit and yogurt and then went inside to make a cup of tea and toast. Returning with her tray, she smiled at the busyness of the small bird population. There were wagtails in abundance, switching their little tails from side to side as they snapped up insects from the lawn.

Half an hour later, Tessa blocked a yawn. She stood, scattering the residue of toast crumbs for the birds. She was out on her feet but at least she'd been able to wind down enough to encourage sleep.

'Hey! Come on, sleepyhead. Wakey-wakey!'

Tessa made a groggy sound from under the bedclothes. 'What is it?' She raised her head and opened one eye.

Alison clicked her tongue. 'You asked me to give you a call before I went to work.'

'What time is it?'

'Two-thirty. I'm just off.'

'Mmm, OK. Any mail?'

'Postcard from your parents from Switzerland. When are they due back?'

'Another three weeks or so.' Tessa hauled herself up against the pillows and blinked. 'Are you just off?'

Alison rolled her eyes. 'Just said I was. Coffee's made and there's a salad in the fridge. Oh, and there's a message from Luke on the answering-machine. Can he bring anything for tonight?'

Tessa groaned. 'Don't you dare say anything at work,' she warned.

'Would I?' Alison looked offended. Turning at the door, she looked back and grinned. 'Remember, now, Tess, whatever you and Luke get up to, be good at it.' Chuckling, she dodged the pillow Tessa threw after her.

Tessa heard the front door close on her friend's soft laughter. Tenting her knees under the sheet, she linked her arms around them and gave in to a dreamy smile. Suddenly the day seemed full of sunshine and promise.

Purposefully, Tessa sprang out of bed. She had a dozen things to organise before Luke arrived.

Luke's heart was trampolining as he brought his car to a stop outside Tessa's house. He'd almost forgotten what it felt like to have these gut-wrenching feelings about a woman. Closing and locking the door, he huffed a self-derisive laugh. On the other hand, maybe he'd just never met a woman like Tessa O'Malley before.

She opened the door before he could knock. 'Hi.' His voice was rough-edged, husky. He swallowed unevenly, just the sight of her causing his nerve-ends to pinch, screwing his muscles tight.

Her hair, mahogany-rich and shot with highlights, tumbled around her shoulders. Her face had a freshly scrubbed look about it, her skin glowing, her mouth redder without lipstick.

She looked impossibly young.

'Hi, yourself.' She smiled, drawing him inside. 'These for me?' She took the flat box of chocolates he was holding out a bit awkwardly. 'Mmm.' She narrowed her gaze on the label. 'Dark chocolates. Lovely. Come through.'

'I vetoed wine,' Luke said, following her along the hall to the lounge room. 'And I couldn't find the flowers I wanted.'

'Oh?' Her head tilted to one side, Tessa regarded him quizzically. 'And what flowers would they be, Doctor?'

'Irises.' He reclaimed the slim gold box of chocolates from her unresisting hands and slipped them onto the sideboard. 'I rather fancied some of those vivid blue ones,' he stated, gently drawing her into his arms. 'But there were none to be had.'

Tessa's heart began clamouring. 'Why irises?'

'Because they're exotic and different...' His fingers curled in the lustrous warmth of her hair. 'And brave-looking somehow with their tall, straight stems. I've missed you, Tess.'

'And I've missed you.' She burrowed against him, loving the feeling of being close to him after what seemed like weeks of uncertainty. She tilted her head back. 'You're early.'

'Mmm.' His mouth lowered to her throat, his lips on the tiny pulse point that beat frantically beneath her chin. 'I booted the patients out of Casualty. Told them to come back tomorrow.'

'As if,' she murmured, and felt his smile on her skin.

'There were times when I thought this moment would never happen.' He drew back to look at her, running the tip of his finger across the soft curve of her bottom lip.

'But it has.' Her throat was so dry she could hardly speak. 'You said we needed to talk,' she said huskily. 'Would you like to do that now or…?'

He looked at her for a long moment, unable to tear his eyes away from the soft mistiness of hers. 'I'd prefer *or*, I think…' His voice caught as he swallowed.

Tessa's heart beat so heavily she could feel it inside her chest. 'Luke…?'

He nodded, seeming to understand what she was asking. Placing his hands beneath her elbows, he lifted her off her feet as though she weighed no more than a feather, his mouth tasting hers over and over. 'Tess…'

'Yes?'

'Let's go to bed.' He gently lowered her to the floor and she walked ahead of him into the bedroom.

They didn't bother with lamps, since none were needed. The soft light of early evening fingered the pale walls and ceiling. Outside the window a wood dove called to its mate and a burst of cicada drumming drenched the stillness.

'This is right, isn't it, Luke?' Her voice was faintly uncertain without the reassurance of his touch.

He stilled. 'Come here.'

She went into his arms and he gathered her in against him. Then he stepped back and, without taking his eyes away from her face, slowly ran his hand down between her breasts, unbuttoning her simple little cotton dress, slipping his hands underneath it, sliding it in one movement from her shoulders.

Then he was tugging off his own clothes and drawing her down with him onto the bed. She shivered, wrapping her bare legs around his, her arms reaching up to pull his head down, sighing as she felt the slick of his skin against hers, felt his body tensing with the effort to control it. For just a second she snapped back to reality. 'Luke, have you come prepared?'

She felt his smile against her mouth. 'Regular Boy Scout.'

And then passion, longing and need took over and Tessa gave up caring about anything, knowing only that they fitted perfectly together and that she was with a man who understood about tenderness.

She gave herself fully, trusting Luke as she'd never trusted any man. And he didn't fail her, taking her on a voyage of discovery where longing and need became loving and giving and where finally, rapturously, he drowned them both in an ocean of total and tumultuous union.

Later, as they lay drowsily replete, Luke turned on his side so that they were facing each other. Lifting a hand lazily, he combed his fingers back through her hair. 'It'll be dark soon.'

'Mmm.'

He gave her a look from under half-closed lids. 'Want me to nip out and get some champagne?'

Freeing a hand, Tessa ran a finger along his jaw and into the cleft in his chin. 'I have some on ice already.'

His eyes softened. 'That certain, were you, Tess?'

'Certain we'd be good together?' She gave a slight, shaky laugh. 'Yes. Weren't you?'

He bent, brushing her lips once and again. 'From the first moment I saw you.'

Tessa raised herself slightly and blinked. 'In the rain?'

'In the rain,' he echoed drily. 'I couldn't get to sleep that night for thinking about you.'

'I thought *you* were an arrogant pig.' Tessa bit her lips on a smile of remembrance.

'I like pigs!' He gave a soft chuckle, pressing his forehead to hers. 'When did you change your mind about me?' He half spanned her waist with one hand, stroking a lazy pattern on her skin.

'Can't remember.' She burrowed in against him. 'I think you kind of just grew on me.'

'Like moss.' He laughed, his breath stirring her hair. Then the laughter stilled in his throat and he looked at her, raw emotion carved into his features. 'You've turned me inside out, Tess... You're incredible.' His voice held the slightest wonder. 'In every way.'

Tessa blinked rapidly, feeling tears of reaction spring into her eyes. Was this Luke's way of telling her he loved her? Filled with joy at the discovery, yet at the same time terribly uncertain, she said throatily, 'That makes two of us, then.'

'Ah, Tess!' He wrapped his arms around her, cradling her head on his chest. He realised his heart was churning. He'd never felt so in touch with another human being in his life. Slowly, he drew her head up until her gaze was level with his. 'So, what are we saying here?' he murmured, tasting her throat and her ear lobe. 'That this is serious business between us?'

Oh, she hoped so. Prayed so. Because she loved him. Loved him in every way a woman should love a man. Loved and trusted him. And would do for the rest of her life.

'I'd say so…' Her words spun out on a little sigh, before he slowly and with exquisite sweetness claimed her lips.

This time their passion was less demanding and they made love slowly and with great care and tenderness. Their soft, teasing murmurs sprinkled the silence until the fire of their passion reignited, driving them before it until there was no escape and they tumbled to a blinding oneness, wrapped in each other's arms.

'I guess I'd better limit my champagne intake to only one glass,' Tessa said ruefully. They'd showered and returned to some sense of reality.

'Pity.' With a suitable flourish, Luke filled her best crystal flutes. 'What are we drinking to?'

Tessa bit her lip. To drink to the future would be too uncertain, too presumptuous. 'Your call.'

'Well, then.' He frowned for a moment, looking down into his glass. Then, as if he'd cleared something in his mind, he lifted his glass to hers. 'To the sweetness of today,' he said with a slow, sexy smile.

'Oh.' She looked up at him, sudden tears welling in her eyes. 'That's lovely.'

And so was their meal.

'I've made lemon chicken with garlic potatoes.' Tessa went about the kitchen, her feet working automatically and her heart alight with happiness. 'I just have to quickly steam the green beans.'

'Ah.' Luke chuckled. 'We're getting all our vitamins, I see.'

She wrinkled her nose at him. 'I happen to have a nice herb and veg patch, that's all. Seems a pity not to make the most of it.' She sought something in a top cupboard. 'Would you do the honours and light the candles, please?'

'I think I can manage that.' With a sharp reflex action, Luke caught the box of matches she tossed to him.

Several minutes later, Tessa proudly brought the big oval serving platter to the table.

Luke shook his head. 'This looks wonderful, Tess.' He looked across at her, his expression soft. 'You continue to astound me.'

Brows raised, she responded laughingly, 'Because I can cook?'

He grinned. 'That's just an added bonus.'

With soft smiles, testament to their new intimacy, they toasted each other again, this time with mineral water.

'Mind if we talk shop for a minute?' Luke asked, when they were sitting over coffee and his chocolates.

'Go ahead.' Snuggling in beside him on the lounge, Tessa offered him her whole attention.

'Doug Tanner came in today to have his stitches removed.' Seeing her frown, Luke clarified, 'Our chap with the dogbite.'

'Oh, of course.' Tessa flapped a hand in recall. 'Was everything OK?'

'He's healing nicely but I've given him another week off. Seeing the kind of work he does, we can't risk an infection at this stage. All that was fine, but we had time for quite a chat.' Luke's mouth compressed for a moment. 'He told me the council has won a government grant to establish a new recreational park that will include quite an extensive forest walk as well.'

Tessa looked faintly puzzled. 'Well, that's great for the town and the district, but why of special interest to me, exactly?'

His mouth quirked. 'Not to you, but I wondered whether Sue's husband might be interested.' He rocked his hand. 'From what you told me, it would seem the kind of work he wants to get into.'

'Luke, that's brilliant!' Tessa beamed up at him. 'They're bound to be taking on extra staff.'

'And Doug says there's to be quite an emphasis on environmental harmony—it could be a very rewarding job to be involved in.'

'And right up Iain's alley.' She flashed him a triumphant grin and then sobered. 'You've really taken this community to your heart, haven't you?'

Luke gave an embarrassed laugh. 'Don't go overboard, Tess. For the present I happen to be working here, that's all.'

Tessa looked away. Whatever Luke said, his action spoke louder than his professed air of uninvolvement with the people of Cressbrook. Wisely, she decided to keep that opinion to herself.

Instead, she said brightly, 'I'll pop a note through the Mitchells' letterbox about what's happening with the council. Iain can follow it up if he's interested. Of course, they may have other plans in mind when they come back from their holiday.'

'In that case, no harm done.' Luke shrugged. 'But if Iain's seriously looking for a change of direction, he could get in on the ground floor.'

'Mmm.' She flashed him her best and brightest smile. 'With the possibility of a nice positive result for one little family-to-be.' She broke off and bit her lip. 'What?'

'You, Tessa O'Malley.' His eyes caressed her tenderly. 'Just you.'

Slowly, their evening drew to a close.

'Are you going to try for a bit more shut-eye before you go on duty?' Luke sent her a questioning, crooked smile.

'Perhaps...' They stood achingly close to each other. 'Perhaps not.'

'Everything about this feels right, doesn't it?'

'Yes...' Tessa was dizzy with the newness of it.

Luke felt the passion within her and wound his arms more tightly around her, amazed at the way their bodies called to one another, how every dip and curve in her willowy suppleness found a home in his.

'Go home,' she whispered, and gave him a little push towards the door. 'You need your sleep, too.'

He reached out a finger, his touch feather-like

along her jaw, her throat and into the soft hollow of her collarbone. 'When will I see you again?'

'At work?'

'No, I meant *see*.' The words came out on a husky growl as his lips travelled from her mouth to the lobe of her ear. 'It's not going to be easy, is it? With me at the residence and you with your housemate.'

Tessa shook her head wordlessly, her throat tight. 'We'll think of something...' She buried her head against his shoulder.

As Tessa walked into A and E for her shift of night duty, an involuntary smile crept up on her. She had a lover. She had love. She had Luke...

Drew McIntosh was right on time for handover. 'Not too busy. Eighty-year-old female, Moira Clifford, brought in from the retirement village, suspected pneumonia. She's just gone up. We're still trying to track down family.' He consulted his notes and then did a double-take back at her as he uttered a suppressed, 'Hey up!'

'What?' Tessa blinked.

'You, Sister O'Malley.' Drew's eyes had a musing gleam. 'No one in the middle of a stint of night duty is supposed to look that good.'

Tessa gave him a sugary smile. 'Must be my new anti-wrinkle cream.'

'Not what I heard...' Drew's voice had a sing-song quality. 'But your secret is safe with me, Tess.' Grinning, he touched the side of his nose.

'That's all right, then,' Tessa said airily. 'Because if I hear any gossip in this place, I'll know where it started, won't I?'

Drew chuckled, undaunted. Winding up the report, he said cheerfully, 'Brad's on duty. I have to admit that lad's come a long way in a short time. Since Luke arrived, probably.' He sent her an arch look. 'Would you agree?'

'I would...' Tessa replied a little huskily. 'Luke seems to have had quite an influence on most people.'

After she'd come off duty at seven the next morning, Tessa hung back, waiting for Luke. And then she heard his voice and her heart fluttered. She hurried to find him.

Luke couldn't believe how energised he felt this morning. And he couldn't stop smiling. Hell, he felt like a teenager in love. That thought brought him up short.

'Luke!'

He turned and saw Tessa coming towards him.

He bustled her straight into his office.

'Good morning...' His smile was tender. 'I thought you'd be long gone.'

Tessa shook her head. 'I was waiting for you.'

'Oh.' He frowned a bit. The 'morning after' was tailor-made for regrets. Was she having them now? Hell, he hoped not. 'You OK?'

Her mouth curved. 'Very OK. You?'

'Come here...' He reached out and hugged her against him. 'I'll show you how OK I am.'

The kiss started gently but in a second they were on fire for each other. Luke growled deep in his throat and lifted his head. 'I need you, Tess,' he said raggedly.

She cupped his face with both hands. 'I need you, too. But you have patients, Doctor. And I'm going home to sleep.'

'So,' he pressed, wearing a crooked smile, 'was this just a bit of sneaky monkey business to get me revved?'

She laughed softly. 'Didn't take much, did it? But, no, that's not what I came for.'

'Now I'm crushed.' His mouth brushed against hers. 'What, sweet Tess, did you want me for, then?'

'Sorry, but I have to talk about work.' Her tone was rueful. 'And I wanted to tell you personally that John Abbott wandered in last night.'

'Ah!' He fixed her with a meaningful gaze. 'How did he seem?'

'A bit ratty, actually. But he came here—that's the main thing. Brad followed your instructions to the letter. It's all in John's notes.' Her brow rose in query. 'How long will you keep him in?'

'Depends.' Luke parked himself on the edge of his desk and folded his arms. 'We don't know yet how he'll respond to the treatment.'

Tessa's mouth turned down wryly. 'I can't explain it, but I'm feeling positive about John. And as soon as he's up to it, I'm going to whisk him along to the kids' ward.'

'You're going to get him painting with them?' Luke smiled, acknowledging their shared understanding of what John Abbott's recovery could possibly involve.

'There has to be some therapeutic benefits from interacting with children and John has so much talent to share…' She trailed away.

Luke gave a nod of understanding and agreement. 'I'll check on him shortly, and let you know.'

He slid off the desk. 'I need a hug before you go.'

Her heart gave an extra thud, and she went straight into his arms.

CHAPTER NINE

THREE weeks later, on a Wednesday, Delia O'Malley was discharged from hospital.

Tessa's parents had arrived in Cressbrook the night before. She'd thought about inviting Luke to join them for dinner but then rejected the idea, deciding that what they had together was still too new, too fragile to share with anyone—even her beloved parents, Tom and Claudia O'Malley.

However, it was a different matter, when they came to the hospital to collect Del. 'Luke wants a word.' Tessa, who was on a day shift, met them in Reception.

'Well, I should think so,' her father said heartily. 'I want a word with him, too. Need to thank him for all he's done for your grandmother.'

Tessa's nerves tightened. 'He's in his office. We can go along now, if you like.'

'Lead on, darling.' Her mother smiled. 'The sooner we get Del home and settled in, the better for everyone.'

Her heart thumping, Tessa knocked on Luke's door and popped her head in. 'My parents are here.' She heard her own voice oddly strangled. 'OK to come in?'

'Of course.' Luke got to his feet. 'Mr and Mrs O'Malley.' Luke's handshake was firm. 'Have a seat, won't you?'

* * *

Almost an hour later, Tessa and Luke waved off the O'Malley clan. 'Well, that went off pretty well,' Luke said, as they made their way back to the A and E department.

Tessa's mouth turned down. She couldn't expect Luke to be aware of the underlying tensions she'd picked up between her parents and grandmother. 'I got the feeling Del wasn't all that happy about having to go to Brisbane to recuperate.'

'Did you?' He looked surprised.

'Mmm.' Frowning slightly, Tessa shoved her hands into the side pockets of her trousers. 'Del would rather have gone home to Half Moon.'

'Well, I don't doubt your powers of perception, Tess, but even you can see that your grandmother can't manage on her own just now.'

'But later on, in the future?' She looked at him hopefully.

Luke lifted a shoulder. 'If she keeps up her physio and her general health remains good, she'll probably be able to come back.'

'She has lifelong friends here. It'll be hard for her, living away from everything she's known.'

'Tess, it's not for ever,' Luke cajoled softly. 'And I think you're underestimating Del. She's gutsy and she'll do whatever it takes.'

Tessa bit her lip. 'Perhaps I could have done more.'

He snorted inelegantly. 'You did magnificently. Holding down a full-time demanding job, spending most of your off-duty hours with Del—'

'Not all of them,' she interrupted with a soft laugh.

'No,' he agreed in a low voice. 'It's been ages, Tess.' His suddenly brooding gaze raked her face.

Tessa held her head at an angle, her heart nearly beating itself out of her chest. 'I, um, thought I'd go out to the farm on the weekend just to air the house and stuff. Care to come?' The invitation was slightly breathless, earnest with her own need.

They'd stopped just inside the casualty entrance and their eyes met, their message clearer than words. Luke raised a hand to stroke his jaw, as if considering his options.

Watching him, Tessa's heart plummeted. Had she come across as too organised, too calculating? Pushing their relationship too hard?

'Are we staying the night?'

She nodded, feeling relief rush through her. 'I— If you'd like to.'

'Silly question.' His eyes crinkled in soft amusement. 'I can be there by late afternoon on Saturday.'

'Good…' She clenched her hands in her pockets to stop herself racing straight into his arms. 'You know the way.'

Luke's mouth turned down at the corners. 'Will my posh car survive the journey, though?'

'It had better.' She slanted him a smile, content to devour him with her eyes.

'Uh-oh.' Turning his head, Luke blew out a resigned breath. 'No peace for the no-chance-to-be-wicked by the look of it.'

'What?' Tessa gave herself a mental shake as Gwyneth hurried up to them.

'The ambulance base has just been on to us.' The young nurse caught her hands together, working them agitatedly. 'They're bringing in ten kids from a school camp. Suspected food poisoning.'

Luke swore. 'OK, we'll need all hands on deck. Let's just hope we don't get another emergency on the back of this one. What's the ETA?'

Gwyneth frowned. 'I'm not sure, but the base said they have to come from Barron Gap Falls.'

'That's only about ten k's out,' Tessa supplied briskly. 'They should be here shortly. Do we know the age group, Gwyneth?' As charge, she was already running over a procedural plan in her head.

'They're from the high school.'

'Right.' Tessa breathed a sigh of relief. At least with an older age group, they could expect some degree of co-operation and sensible answers from the kids. But on the other hand, if they were terribly ill…

Within minutes Cressbrook's two ambulances arrived, followed by one of the teachers who had offered his Land Cruiser to transport young patients to the hospital.

Tessa could see at once that the students were quite ill, some of them glassily pale. She blew out a controlling breath. They were going to take some sorting out. That was certain.

As the teenagers came streaming in, some walking, some on stretchers, Gwyneth turned helplessly to Tessa. 'We're going to run out of cubicles!'

'Then we'll put some of the students in the side ward.' Tessa forced patience into her voice. 'And be ready with basins, please, in case they're still vomiting.'

'Oh, yuck…' Gwyneth's suppressed revulsion left Tessa boiling inside.

Lord, stop me from slapping her, she implored silently.

'Right, people,' Luke came in authoritatively, 'let's get some triage, shall we?' He half turned his head. 'Tessa?'

She ran her eyes over the assembled group. 'This is going to need everyone's co-operation. Some of the students appear quite ill so Wendy, where you can, would you start taking names, please? And liaise with the accompanying teacher about letting the parents know—'

'How do we work this, patient-wise?' Brad cut in, throwing the question at Luke.

'We'll see the kids on stretchers first. You team with Gwyneth. Anything you're uncertain about, don't dither. Give me a yell. Now, let's go.'

Accompanied by Luke, Tessa went into the first cubicle. Their patient, a seventeen-year-old female student, looked pale and clammy. Bending over the stretcher, Tessa asked, 'What's your name, honey?'

'Jody Singer.'

'And when did you start feeling ill, Jody?' Tessa smoothed the girl's long blonde hair away from her forehead.

'Soon after breakfast.' She bit her lips together and went on. 'The other kids were sick, too.'

'Jody,' Luke came in gently, 'I just need to feel your tummy.' His mouth compressed as he palpated. 'Right.' He stepped back and drew the sheet up. 'That's fine. Have you had any diarrhoea?'

'Some. Oh-h…'

Tessa noticed the student's pallor. 'Do you want to vomit, Jody?'

The girl blocked a tear with the palm of her hand and sniffed. 'I feel awful.' She swallowed convulsively and tried to sit up. 'My sister's really sick...'

Tessa squeezed her hand. 'It's OK, sweetie. Don't worry. She'll be looked after.'

'Take it easy, Jody.' Luke began scribbling on the chart. 'We'll have you feeling much better soon.'

'Oh, help,' the youngster gulped, and gave a little moan. 'I want to be sick...'

Tessa grabbed a basin. They were in for a morning and a half with this lot!

'Someone's head should roll over this.' Luke was grim-faced. 'Let's run ten milligrams of Maxolon, stat, please, Tessa. That should settle her tummy.'

Quickly, Tessa secured the drip and taped it down. 'Lomotil for the diarrhoea?'

Luke nodded. 'Let's start with two orally and cut back to one after each bowel movement.' He frowned. 'She's dehydrating. I'd like her on four per cent glucose and one-fifth normal saline IV. Sips of water only. Could you take her blood sugar levels as well, please? Anything below three, I need to know about it.'

And so it went on for the next couple of hours.

'I don't know about you, but I'm starving.' Luke followed Tessa into the staffroom. They'd just done a ward round, rechecking all their young patients.

Tessa glanced at her watch and pulled a face. 'We're too late for the canteen. They'll be reduced to selling chocolate bars and crisps by now.'

Luke rolled his eyes. 'Let's see what your magic

cupboard can produce, then, Sister. This guy's in need of sustenance.'

Tessa held up a can of baked beans and he shuddered.

'Please! Not after the morning we've just had.'

She made a few more suggestions, which he vetoed, and then she clicked her fingers. 'I brought in some savoury rice yesterday. Now, if the night shift hasn't snaffled it… Ah! Still intact.'

'Brilliant.' He fell into a chair and let his breath go in a long exhalation.

'It doesn't look like any of the students will need to be admitted, does it?' Tessa placed the container in the microwave and punched a button.

'I'm still a bit concerned about Jody's sister, Rebecca.' Luke furrowed a hand through his hair. 'But at least I've managed to get some response from the Health Department. A couple of officers are on their way from Brisbane as we speak.'

'That was quick.' Tessa opened the door of the microwave, gave the rice a final stir and put it back.

Luke's laugh was short and wry. 'I called in a favour.'

Tessa piled their plates with the piping-hot, fluffy rice. 'It's got loads of veg.' She put the plate down in front of him.

'Any prawns?' Luke forked a path hopefully through the broccoli and red peppers.

Tessa cocked a brow at him. 'No prawns.'

'It's good,' he admitted a few minutes later, setting about the food with obvious relish.

'Don't sound so surprised. Any idea what may

have caused the food poisoning? Sorry.' She shuddered gently. 'Probably not a good time to ask.'

'I'd guess it was something they ate for breakfast, seeing they were ill soon after. The Health Department guys will suss it out, send whatever they come up with for analysis. In the meantime, the camp will be cut short, I believe.' He pulled a face as his beeper went off.

'Shout if you need me.'

'Roll on Saturday.' He had his hand on the swing door almost before the words were uttered.

Tessa was relieved to hand over to Sue, who was back from holiday, at the end of the shift. In more ways than one it had been a taxing kind of day.

'So…' Sue looked keenly at her counterpart. 'All the students have now been discharged, I take it?'

'All but one.' Tessa referred to her notes. 'A fourteen-year-old, Rebecca Singer. Luke wants to keep her overnight. She was seriously dehydrated. Still on a drip actually, but she's perked up and I imagine she'll be released in the morning.' Tessa blocked a yawn. 'It's all on the charts anyhow—or in the computer if you're so minded.'

'Right.' Sue changed tack brightly. 'Your gran went home today, didn't she?'

'Mmm.' Tessa chewed her lip. 'Well, not home exactly. Mum and Dad took her home with them to Brisbane. She needs to keep up her physio.'

'But she'll be back, won't she?'

'Oh, yes,' Tessa said, a bit too heartily. 'Luke seems to think so—well, when I pushed him,' she admitted with a wry little smile. 'But what about you?' Tessa leaned forward with a grin. 'Do I detect an air of excitement about you, Mrs Mitchell?'

Sue hiccuped a laugh. 'Iain's on the short-list for one of the council jobs for the new environmental park.'

'That's brilliant! Tell him congratulations from me.'

'Thanks, Tess, I'll do that. But Iain hasn't got it yet,' Sue cautioned.

'But he must have made a good impression. I heard dozens applied for the four jobs that were going.'

'We did a fairly professional-looking CV,' Sue admitted happily. 'Listed everything he's ever done workwise.'

Tessa lifted a shoulder. 'Well, that's what these career advisers tell you to do, isn't it? Personally, I think he'll walk it.'

'Oh, gosh, I hope so…'

'You're feeling OK, aren't you?' Tessa asked gently. 'The baby?'

'The baby's fine. But we've a lot hanging on this job. It will mean security for us if Iain gets it and I'll be able to cut back to part time.'

Tessa patted her friend's hand. 'He'll get it. I have a very good feeling about this.'

Sue chuckled. 'You and your feelings! Next thing you'll be telling me you weave spells.'

Tessa tapped her nose and tried to look mysterious. 'All zee time.'

How Del must be pining for this, Tessa thought, a little dip in her heart. She'd arrived at Half Moon just after eight on Saturday morning and had taken herself off on a tour of the garden.

The place was a riot of colour. Catching hold of a lavender bush, she buried her nose in the sweet-smelling blossom, recalling how Del liked to cut and dry the flowers each season and sew them into little muslin sachets to place amongst her underclothes and linen.

This year it would be down to her, Tessa decided. In fact, she might even make a start today, before Luke arrived. The thought of having him here, in this her most special place, caused a dreamy smile to play over her lips as she anticipated their imminent re-union.

Making her way across to the timber fence, she placed her hands on the top rail, looking down over the valley. And gradually moment by moment the magic of the countryside renewed her spirit, ener-gised her body.

Humming a tune she'd heard on the radio that morning, she went into the house and spent the next couple of hours vacuuming and polishing the old ce-dar furniture, toiling over the heavy round dining table until it shone. She smiled wryly, giving the back of each chair a final swipe with her polishing cloth. They didn't quite match but they were as much a part of her family as the lion-claw-foot bath.

And speaking of that, she closed her eyes and took a little breath. Luke was in for the surprise of his life.

Almost dusk.

The orange and gold flush on the clouds indicated the day was sliding away. And Tessa, dressed in jeans and a soft, checked shirt, sat on the faded swing seat on the verandah. Luke had phoned earlier. He was on his way.

He had to be up-front with her. Luke passed through the last set of gates and began to climb up the bony ridge of road to the Half Moon homestead.

He looked ruefully at his hands clenched on the steering-wheel and immediately loosened his grip. Good grief! He should be handling things much better than this.

But the fact remained that he wasn't. Tessa O'Malley was everything he wanted in a woman and each time he thought about her—which was practically every waking minute—his mind became a jumbled mess. But one thing flew clear.

He ached for her.

Tessa's nerves were shredding. She'd seen Luke's car, its hood glinting in the last rays of the sun. Now that he was almost here… She wrapped her arms around her body, feigning cold. What if this time it was all terribly awkward between them? She'd die of embarrassment. No. She closed her eyes and took a deep breath. She'd simply *die*.

Gathering her courage, she slid off the swing and went to the front gate to wait for him. She frowned. He seemed to be taking an age to get out of the car.

For a terrible moment Luke thought he was going to have to greet her in his state of heightened awareness. Feeling like a kid on a first date, he played for time, removing his sunglasses and folding them back in their case, riffling through the glove box for nothing in particular.

When he had himself in check, he swung out of

the car. 'No Sheppy?' He squirmed at the inanity of his greeting.

'He's living with Brendan these days.' Tessa opened the gate and waited for him. 'No problems on the way up?'

'No.' Luke took the last few steps towards her. 'Hi.'

Tessa's heart was swooping like a drunken butterfly. 'Hello.' She met his eyes, a shy smile playing over her lips, and Luke suddenly knew he'd crack wide open if he didn't kiss her.

He held out his arms and she flew into them. Wrapping herself tightly around him, she pressed her body against him and turned her face up for his kiss.

'Tess…' A gravelly sigh dragged itself up from the depths of his chest, and his mouth took hers as if he were dying of thirst.

She shifted against him, each tiny movement a subtle invitation for him to hold her more tightly, more intimately.

And he did.

Heat exploded in him and he gave a strangled groan, her soft pleas driving him close to the edge. 'Tessa, wait…' Somehow, he found just enough control to gather her up and carry her inside to one of the bedrooms.

'So this is Tessa O'Malley's girlhood bedroom,' Luke surmised, as they lay, warmly entwined, waiting for their breathing to return to normal.

'Except for the addition of the double bed, basically untouched since I was about thirteen.' A dreamy expression on her face, Tessa lay back in the crook of his arm.

Almost hungrily, Luke's gaze swept over the youthful collection of knick-knacks, posters and photographs. Amusement came into his eyes. 'You were into *Abba*?'

'All little girls were!'

'And dolls!' His eyebrows soared. 'Tess, there have to be two dozen of them on that shelf.'

'So what?' Tessa chuckled. 'Maybe I'm keeping them for *my* daughter.'

Now there was a thought. A thought that led to a road paved with dynamite. Tilting her face towards him, Luke gently kissed her on the mouth. 'So…sweet Tessa, when do we get to share that magnificent bath?'

'Whenever you like.' She gave a breathless little laugh. 'I should warn you, I've, um, set the scene rather grandly.'

He gave her a rakish grin. 'Candles?'

'Scented. And towels—all warm and fluffy.'

'Mmm… Wine?'

'A full-bodied red—very smooth.'

'What else?' he murmured, his mouth roaming over her cheek, her throat and into the valley between her breasts.

'Grapes—lusciously juicy.'

'Chilled?'

'Naturally.'

'I can't wait.'

'Neither can I…' Almost in slow motion, she lifted a hand, running her forefinger over his mouth until he parted it and bit gently on her nail. 'Luke,' she whispered on a jagged little breath, running her hands up through his hair.

Luke lowered his head and they kissed slowly, completely. Until kissing was no longer enough.

They left their departure as late as they could on Sunday, going back to the creek for a picnic lunch but this time driving in Tessa's Jeep.

'I've never been so happy,' Tessa said softly, her face dappled by the canopy of leaves. They had eaten their crusty bread rolls stuffed with ham and salad and were lying back on the rug-covered groundsheet.

Beside her, Luke sensed her need for him to reciprocate. But he couldn't. Instead, his gut clenched with a huge uncertainty. Even closing his eyes and listening to the murmur of the creek mingling with the dozing hum of cicadas failed to iron out the lead weight in his chest.

'Hey, you!' Tessa put out a hand and nudged him in the ribs. 'What about a walk before we head back?'

'Sounds good.' Luke grabbed at the reprieve. Anything to postpone the talk they still hadn't got around to. 'Did you play here a lot as a child?'

'All the time.' Their footsteps took them under the fringe of lacy willows that ran along the bank of the creek and for a moment they stood and watched a dragonfly skim the surface of the water. 'Caught tadpoles, too,' she reminisced with a smile, 'over there.' She pointed to where the creek widened into a clear-bottomed pool beside a sandy bank.

'I've never caught a tadpole in my life.' He laughed, hugging her more closely to his side.

After a while they left the creek and made their way through the thick tussocky grass. Luke lifted his head, inhaling. The pungent smell of haymaking was in the air, along with the drone of a tractor. 'It seems to me farmers never get a day off,' he observed.

Tessa made a moue. 'Farming has always been governed by the seasons. In the busy times, it's seven days a week— Oh!' She stopped with a little cry and bent forward to part a clump of tall grass. 'Look! It's a quail! Are you hurt, baby? It's a little female.'

'How can you tell?' Watching intently, Luke hunkered down beside her.

'She's brown and speckled for the most part.' Tessa pulled the tussock wider so he could see more clearly. 'The males have a much darker plumage around the head.'

'Do you think she's injured?'

'Quite possibly.' Tessa didn't attempt to touch the bird. 'She's quite young, too, and obviously out of her territory.'

'Are we supposed to do something?' Luke frowned as the bird's wings began to whirr and pump in the grass.

Without looking up, Tessa snapped out her hand towards him. 'Give me your jumper, Luke.'

He stared blankly for a second. 'Are you cold?'

'Not me!' She gave a short laugh. 'I'm going to use it to pick up our little feathered friend here. But birds are easily over stressed so I need to keep my movements very slow and careful…'

Luke looked doubtful. 'Just watch out it doesn't bite you for your trouble.'

'Not this baby.' Deftly, as though she'd done it a

dozen times before, Tessa gently placed Luke's jumper over the quail and lifted it out of the grass. It made a feeble attempt to flutter and then quietened.

Luke straightened, aware of an odd feeling of unreality. The little quail's bright eyes were staring straight ahead but she seemed content enough to be held. He sent Tessa a tender look. 'Now what, Mrs Doolittle?'

She smiled briefly. 'We'll have to see what can be done for this youngster.'

They walked the short distance back to the Jeep. Following Tessa's instructions, Luke found a carton in the boot and folded back the lid, anchoring it while Tessa placed the injured bird inside.

He hesitated before closing it. 'Shouldn't we give it some water or something?'

'Uh-uh.' Tessa shook her head. 'Until we know what kind of injury it has, the golden rule is nil by mouth. Otherwise water forced into a bird can end up in its lungs.'

'So basically it drowns.' Luke shook his head. 'Why didn't I know that?'

Tessa held the box while he opened the rear door of the Jeep. 'Because you're a people doctor, not a vet?' she volunteered with a grin. She handed him the carton and he placed it carefully on the back seat.

'I know I keep asking.' Luke closed the door with a gentle click. 'But what happens now?'

'I'll call in at the police station when we get back to town.' Tessa tossed her keys to him. 'They'll have a list of volunteer wildlife carers. This little creature will be safe and sound with one of them by tonight.'

Luke gave a dry laugh as they piled into the front

seat. 'And there I was about to fancy myself as anaesthetist to your veterinary skills.'

She showed him the tip of her tongue. 'Do you mind waiting a bit to get your jumper back? It's better if we leave the bird alone now to get over its fright.'

'Do I have a choice?' But he sounded philosophical. 'Just be thankful I wasn't wearing my best Arran.'

Tessa laughed and then said teasingly, 'You'd have lent it to me anyway—wouldn't you?' She reached up to stroke his face, then sighed as his lips fell softly against her mouth and clung there. His face was faintly, deliciously rough. He hadn't shaved that morning. 'Mmm…' she murmured, nuzzling his chin. 'Designer stubble. I love it…'

And I love *you*. The words stayed locked in Luke's heart and he could think of nothing else.

The next afternoon Tessa came on duty with a wild feeling of joy in her heart.

With shared memories of their weekend still fresh, she found a moment to send Luke a lingering smile. But he seemed ill at ease and quickly looked away.

She frowned, feeling dismissed, but she couldn't know the fever of torment Luke found himself in. He hadn't slept well, his thoughts centring around the fact that his contract finished in less than six weeks. But now, when he thought of leaving, it brought no sense of excitement or relief. Instead, he could think of it only in terms of leaving the most amazing woman he'd ever met.

'We've got the lab results on the food from the

school camp,' he said a bit stiltedly, when they met up at the nurses' station.

'Oh?' Tessa blinked. It all seemed like weeks ago now.

'It was the sausages.' Luke rubbed a finger down his nose. 'Apparently the cook or whoever was in charge of the catering left them out of the fridge overnight to thaw.'

Tessa grimaced. 'A breeding ground for salmonella. Poor kids. What happened to the culprit?'

'I've lodged a report.' He lifted a dismissive shoulder. 'I imagine the rest is up to the school authorities.' His smoky blue gaze turned suddenly brooding. 'Can we talk some time soon?'

'Ah, yes... I suppose.' Tessa felt her pulse rate accelerate, her gaze drawn irresistibly to the stubborn line of his jaw, the sensual, clean-lipped mouth whose exploration had taken her to such dizzying heights when they'd made love. 'Is something wrong?'

'Tess, this isn't the time.'

She bit her lip. He looked uncomfortable, almost hunted. 'Come to the house tomorrow, then. Lunchtime?'

His dark brows rose. 'We'll be alone?'

'Of course.'

CHAPTER TEN

SOMETHING was wrong.

Watching Luke walk away, Tessa felt a lurching sensation of loss in the pit of her stomach. Had he decided to end it between them? But why? When it was all so perfect…

She worked through her shift in a haze of uncertainty. Even though neither of them had actually acknowledged it, she knew they were in love. Totally. She'd never been like this with any other man.

Even the relationship she'd had with Will Carter seemed a pale imitation now she knew what loving someone really meant.

Next day, Tessa waited for Luke to arrive. She'd made sandwiches and coffee, although she doubted whether either of them would be able to eat anything. Her stomach was churning incessantly, and when her doorbell rang just after twelve she nearly jumped out of her skin.

Luke was tight-lipped. He obviously hadn't come straight from work, she decided. He was dressed in battered jeans and a black polo shirt. 'Come in,' she said, and turned back into the room. The front door closed quietly behind Luke and he followed her through to the kitchen. Edgily, he accepted her offer of coffee but refused any food.

Very aware of him beside her, Tessa poured the

two mugs of coffee and handed him one. 'Let's go outside to the pergola.' If he had something awful to say, she'd prefer to deal with it there. 'Do you have to get back to the hospital in a hurry?'

'Ah, no.' His mouth straightened into a hard line. 'I managed to arrange cover for the next couple of hours.'

They sat facing each other across the wooden outdoor table, a heavy silence descending on them with the intensity of a fog rolling in from the sea.

'Tessa, I have to tell you something.' Luke hunched over his mug of coffee.

Tessa dragged in a deep breath. Suddenly she felt as though a trap were about to open and snare her with its ugly teeth. 'Better tell me, then.' She forced her mouth into a smile that felt stiff and uncomfortable.

'I...haven't been quite up-front with you.'

Her heart took a nosedive and then began clamouring. Suddenly she wasn't sure she wanted to hear what he was about to tell her. Had she trusted a man again only to have it blow up in her face? She wound her arms around her midriff, almost as if to shield her body from the expected blow. 'Tell me...'

Luke hesitated, searching for the right words. 'The reasons I came to Cressbrook were not exactly what you gave me credit for. I came because I was forced to,' he said grimly.

Forced to? What did that mean? The words went round and round in her head, thumping intolerably like a physical pain. Her fingers whitened with the pressure of gripping her upper arms. Was he in trouble with the medical board? Or running from something? Oh, lord. She squeezed her eyes shut. Must I hear this?

'I let you go on believing I'd come here out of some kind of public-spirited conscience. The fact was, the only way I could get to America was to take a deal the Health Department cut me. I had to agree to work in rural health for three months before they'd release the funding for my overseas training. I didn't *want* to come to Cressbrook. Hell, I didn't even know where it was!'

Tessa shook her head in disbelief. Drawing sharply back, she looked into Luke's anguished face. 'And that's it?'

'Basically, yes.' His mouth twisted. 'So, you see, Tess, I'm no better than those other locums you held in such contempt. I wasn't exactly dragged here, kicking and screaming, as you so eloquently put it, but when I knew I had no choice but to come here, I was certainly peeved.'

'Peeved!' Tessa didn't know whether to laugh or cry. In fact, she did a bit of both, shaking her head from side to side, her eyes tightly closed. 'Peeved...'

'Tessa, you're not making sense!' Luke's anxiety gave his voice a sharp edge. 'Look, I know I lied by omission—'

'Luke, you idiot! You wonderful, scrupulous idiot!'

'What?' He lifted one broad shoulder impatiently. 'I don't understand.'

Tessa felt as if she were reeling. She sank forward onto the table, clutching her head.

'Look, Tess...' Luke's jaw worked for a moment

before he went on. 'I realise this probably wasn't what you expected to hear…'

Too darned right it wasn't! She smiled up at him, tears welling in her eyes suddenly.

'Tessa, what the hell…?'

She moistened her lips and took a long shuddering breath. 'I thought you were going to tell me you wanted to finish with me!'

There was a long, long silence. Tessa watched the disbelief and puzzlement come and go on his face. Finally, he said, 'Where did you get an idea like that?'

Her eyelashes fluttered down. 'I just did…'

Luke shot to his feet and then he was holding her as if he'd never let her go. 'Ah, Tess…' She felt him shaking. It took her a few seconds to realise he was shaking with laughter.

'Thanks for scaring me half to death!'

'Ah, Tess…'

'Stop saying that!' She thumped him on the back with a small fist.

'I can't believe the knots we tied ourselves in.' He collapsed back against the trunk of a sturdy old eucalypt, taking her with him and wrapping his arms loosely around her. His blue eyes sought hers hungrily. 'Truly, I cannot believe this.'

Her mouth twitched. 'Me neither…'

'I felt so badly about deceiving you, Tess,' he said softly. Lowering his mouth to hers, he teased the corners of her lips until she opened them to him. And kissed him back.

* * *

Later, they sat over fresh coffee and the sandwiches Tessa had made earlier. 'I don't understand,' she said, gazing across the table at him, her chin cupped in her hand. 'Governments have always funded lots of study packages, from the arts to medicine and science. Why were you in such a huff about receiving one—apart from the obvious fact that you had to comply with their conditions, of course?'

A long breath jagged its way from his lungs. 'I've always paid my own way in life. That way I retain control. And I'd saved damned hard for this exact purpose. I've wanted to work in the States for as long as I can remember.'

'So, what happened?' Tessa felt a lick of unease and looked away, busying herself over the coffee-pot.

'My family became financially crippled. I had to help them.' Luke dropped the words like stones into a deep pond.

Tessa's mouth dried. 'Luke, I'm sorry. Honestly, you don't have to tell me your family's business.'

'I know that, Tess.' He flicked a hand impatiently. 'The dust has settled a bit now so I can talk about it without screaming the place down.'

'Is that what you did?'

His harsh laugh cracked out. 'You bet I did. Oh, not to my parents,' he hastened to add. 'But to the boffins who let them down—them and thousands of others.'

Tessa took a careful mouthful of her coffee, her mind spinning. And suddenly what he was referring to began to ring bells everywhere. 'Are we talking about the collapse of that insurance giant last year?

The one that went belly-up and took all their clients' money with them?'

Luke nodded, his mouth tight. 'My dad's name was bandied about in the press. He's one of the state's biggest developers. He employed dozens of people, mostly builders and ancillary workers. He had huge funds invested in that insurance company to cover his employees for their superannuation and long-service entitlements, as well as carrying hefty accident insurance to cover against workplace accidents and so on. He lost the lot and has very little prospect of getting it back. But he felt obliged to try to meet at least some proportion of his workers' severance pay from the company.

'He sold everything and Andre and I kicked in where we could. Even though none of it was Dad's fault, we felt the Stretton name was at stake. And at least we still had jobs. Dad's people had nothing.'

'That must have been awful.' And seeing his own plans go up in smoke must have been awful for him as well, Tessa thought. His pride must have taken a battering. She realised belatedly why he was living at the doctors' residence instead of finding his own accommodation. Luke was all but broke.

'I know what you're thinking, Tess,' he said roughly. 'But I'm over the worst of it now. And there's probably something to be said for not attaching too much importance to worldly goods. My car is all I have left, and I've a buyer for that as soon as I'm ready to leave for the States. I won't starve.' He gave her a crooked grin.

And what about *us*? She picked up her mug with shaking fingers, her insides suddenly twisting as the truth hit. He had his sights set on this next phase of his life and now it seemed painfully obvious he didn't intend to commit to any long-term relationship with her. And she couldn't say he'd deceived her about that. He'd made it clear right from the start just where his future lay…

Her throat closed tightly. She felt caught in a sea of confusion. 'How long will you be away?'

'A year, if I can manage it.' He spanned his fingers carefully around his mug. 'The hospital in Louisville has a specialty unit for transplants. I'm drawn to that.'

'Transplants?' Surprise edged her question.

'Yes.' He looked down briefly. 'Then, hopefully, I'll be able to bring back home what I've learned.'

And obviously make his base in a big teaching hospital somewhere. 'I can see now why you would have thought you were marking time by more or less being forced to come *here*.' Tessa's voice contained a thread of bitterness and he glanced up sharply.

'I believe I've given the hospital my best efforts,' he said stiffly.

The silence between them lengthened and became thicker.

Luke stared at her, just watched her, and then said flatly, 'We're kind of up the creek without a paddle, aren't we, Tess?'

She shrugged, too close to the edge to answer. She couldn't believe how swiftly things between them had broken down. Pain welled in her heart. Slowly, insidiously she felt tentacles surround her heart and squeeze.

Luke's emotions began to show as well. 'Would you consider coming over to join me?'

'As what?' She threw at him harshly. 'Your live-in lover? I don't think so, Luke.'

'You might be able to work,' he said without much conviction. 'You're a fine nurse, Tess.'

Her mouth thinned. 'I probably wouldn't be able to get a green card. And just the thought of the rigmarole involved gives me a headache. I've had friends who went down that road. It takes ages to get accreditation.'

'Granted, it does some thinking outside the square you live in,' he said finally.

And what did that mean when it was at home? 'Anyway, there's Del.' Tessa began clutching at straws to save face, when in reality she was dying inside. 'She's not settling well. I think I'll bring her back, live with her at Half Moon until she's fully fit again.'

Luke frowned. 'How long have you been thinking like this?'

About two minutes. She glanced up at him, unsurprised to see the look of scepticism on his face. 'What does it matter?' Her voice hardened. 'I have commitments here, even if you don't.'

'That's hardly fair, Tessa. You've known all along what my plans were.'

'To take me to bed?' she gave a snort of derision. 'That about sums it up, doesn't it, Luke?'

'It wasn't like that!' he said, his eyes slashing her like lasers. 'It wasn't like that at all! We had something wonderful together.'

Had. Already he was talking in the past tense. Her

throat felt like sandpaper as she swallowed. 'Luke, just go, please. There's no point in talking any further.'

'All right.' His mouth snapped shut, his tightly clamped lips a harsh line across his face.

Tessa stayed motionless at the table until the last sounds of his car had died away.

Luke couldn't believe how badly he'd handled things. He brought the heel of his hand down hard on the steering-wheel. He should have told her he loved her, couldn't do without her. Instead, he'd come on all patronising, offering her that tepid little invitation to join him in the States. Almost insinuating she was insular. No wonder she'd rejected him out of hand.

She'd been right. He'd acted selfishly from the beginning. He'd seen Tessa O'Malley, had wanted her and had reached out for what he'd wanted, accepting what she'd offered without much thought for the future.

Now they were both hurting and it was all a mess. But he still had a bit of time to turn things around. Quite how he didn't know.

She'd just have to tough it out. She'd done it before and she could do it again. Luke was nowhere to be seen. The bitter residue of their last meeting stayed with Tessa as she tapped a report into the computer.

With steely determination, she decided that from now on she'd be her own person, depend on no one. Next weekend, for instance, she wouldn't hang about waiting for any crumbs Luke might want to throw her.

Instead, she'd drive to Brisbane. At least she was sure of a warm welcome from her parents and she could see at first hand how Del was doing.

She chewed softly on her bottom lip, her fingers hovering over the keyboard. From now on, Luke could do what he liked, but she was sure of one thing—there'd be no more invitations to Half Moon.

As the days went on, she began to realise that work was her salvation, the only constant in her life. Painting a bright smile on her face, she hid her grief, interacting with Luke when she absolutely had to. If he looked like hell, that was his problem.

Then ten days later, on a Wednesday, all Tessa's avoidance tactics were wasted—she and Luke were forced together by circumstances beyond their control. When the emergency call came, she went hurriedly to find him.

'Where's the fire?' He seemed to look through her, his face a mask of polite attention.

Tessa swallowed the unprofessional barb. 'We've just had an emergency call from the ambulance base. There's been a fall at the midweek race meeting, several horses and jockeys involved.' She took a deep breath. 'They want a doctor at the scene, stat.'

Luke swore softly. 'In that case, we'd better get out there.'

Tessa's heart did an odd tattoo. 'You want me? I mean, Roz is—'

'I want *you*.' Luke's look was fierce. 'If there are horses involved, I can't think of anyone else I'd want around me.'

So it was all about her ability with horses! Tessa's heart, which had begun soaring, dropped like a wounded bird. 'I'll collect the emergency pack,' she said stiffly.

'We'll take my car.' Luke spun on his heel. 'Bradley!'

White coat flapping, Brad sped out of a nearby treatment room.

'Tessa and I have an emergency at the racecourse.' Luke stripped off his tie as though it was choking him. 'You're in charge. Don't let me down.'

Brad seemed to grow visibly. 'You can count on me, Luke. Good luck!'

Despite the reasons for it, Tessa gave in to a dizzying feeling of *déjà vu* as she swung herself into Luke's low-slung car. She shot him a quick look. 'Do you know where the racetrack is?'

'Five minutes away, isn't it?' He shot out of the parking bay and accelerated towards the street.

'Take the turning opposite Wheatley's garage,' Tessa confirmed, 'and we're almost there.'

Luke put his foot down. 'Poor visibility couldn't have caused this foul-up,' he commented gruffly. It was, in fact a clear, crisp day full of sunshine.

'No.' Tessa shrugged. Offhand, she could think of a number of reasons why the jockeys could have got into difficulties. It took only one horse to stumble. That action could result in a domino effect if the others were following immediately behind.

They were at the country racetrack in a few minutes. His eyes narrowed, Luke accelerated his car through the entrance gates and bumped on up a strip of bitumenised road to the enclosure.

The cheerful rows of bunting around the bookmakers' stands and food tents gave no indication of the drama being played out on the track.

The clerk of the course and a couple of the trainers were endeavouring to secure the horses that had run amok.

'It looks chaotic,' Luke said thinly, as they slammed out of the car.

Tessa caught sight of several of the horses backed against the rails, shivering with fright. One part of her ached to go to them, try to steady them down, but today that wasn't her role.

'Look lively, Tess!' Luke snapped his fingers. He hitched up the emergency pack and they were off at a run.

Both the Cressbrook ambulances were at the scene. 'How many involved?' Luke shot the question at Len Taylor, who was heading the triage.

'Three, Doc. One jockey unconscious, one with a fractured leg and iffy shoulder and one of the apprentices is in a bad way. Could be spleen damage.'

'Right, I'll see him first.'

'Her.' Len looked grim. 'It's Lizzie Collins.'

Tessa gave a gasp of horror. 'Sue's little sister.'

Luke's expression became tight. 'See what you can do for the others, Len. Don't hesitate to use your initiative. I'll back you up. Tess?' he touched her shoulder. 'I'll need you with me.'

Lizzie Collins's face looked glassily pale against the bright green of her riding silks. Luke squatted beside her. 'Get a BP reading, Tess.' He put his hand to the injured girl's wrist and shook his head. 'Barely there.' In a second he was whipping a torch out of the emergency pack. 'Dammit,' he swore softly, 'her pupils are all over the place.' He swung back to Tessa, his gaze widening in question.

She shook her head. 'Seventy over forty.' They both knew they had a crisis on their hands. Very possibly, Lizzie Collins was bleeding internally. Tessa's hands moved in a reflex action, loosening the waistband of Lizzie's jodhpurs so Luke could palpate her stomach.

'We've got problems.' His breath hissed out sharply. 'She's as hard as a rock. Get a line in, Tess. We'll run haemacell, stat, and hope that holds her until we can get her to surgery.'

'Tom Eckhardt's just started on that biker with the lower leg injury.' Tessa's look was uncertain. 'He'll have most of the theatre staff with him.'

'Then I'll have to do Lizzie with whatever help's available. Keep a close eye on her.' Luke shot to his feet. Pulling his mobile out of his back pocket, he punched a logged-in number and waited to be connected.

'Roz? Hi. Could you alert Theatres, please? I'm bringing in an eighteen-year-old female, suspected ruptured spleen. I'll need to do an emergency laparotomy. The patient's bleeding out rapidly so I need priority on all available O-neg. blood and we'll cross-match on arrival.'

'Jill Barnard's the only anaesthetist available today and she's with Tom Eckhardt,' Roz said calmly. 'What do you want to do?'

Luke squeezed the bridge of his nose, thinking quickly. 'Tell Brad to scrub and wait for me. He's had some experience and I can guide him until Jill can take over. And, Roz, have the team ready to meet us in Resus. Haul in another body from somewhere to stand by. Dig someone out of bed if you have to. ETA fifteen minutes.'

Tessa felt a swirl of nervous tension in her stomach. Ideally, Lizzie should have been airlifted to Brisbane. But there was no time. She needed emergency surgery. Thank heaven, Luke had the skills. And what about Sue? A lump formed in Tessa's throat. She didn't need this on top of her own recent scare. But, then, trouble seemed to come in heaps…

'Back in a tick.' Luke grabbed his bag and sprinted across to where the jockey with the suspected broken leg was lying. 'Well handled, folks.' He cast a quick look around. The injured man's shoulder had been supported in a sling and he'd been placed on oxygen. 'Do we have a name?'

'Ryan Hogan.' Len Taylor was at Luke's elbow. 'What do you reckon about the leg, Doc? Fractured NOF?'

'Unquestionably. Would you get a doughnut dressing around that protruding bone, please, Len? He's going to need an open reduction and an internal fixator. We'll Medivac him to Brisbane.'

'I've already called the base on that score,' Len said. 'Chopper's on its way. I figured you'd have enough on your plate with Lizzie here.'

'Thanks, mate.' Luke clapped a hand on the ambulance officer's shoulder. 'We'll need to stabilise your chap for the journey in that case. Let's get him hooked up to some normal saline for starters and I'll give him a jab of morphine to tide him over until he gets to hospital.'

'The other kid, Jason Liddell, has come round. He seems OK,' one of the other ambulance officers reported. 'What do you want to do with him, Doc?'

'Take him straight to Casualty for observation. If he's concussed, we can't be too careful.'

The journey to the hospital with Lizzie was the stuff of nightmares. Both Luke and Tessa rode with her. Luke looked grim. 'Don't take your eyes off her, Tess. How's her BP doing?'

'Still low but she's hanging on. Are you going to take blood?'

'If I can find a vein to give me anything.' Luke snapped on a new pair of gloves. 'It seems criminal when she's barely got enough to keep her going. But we've got to have something to get a cross-match.'

'Sue's on days off.' Tessa's voice cracked. 'But at least all the family's hereabouts. They'll have each other for support.'

Luke's expression was strained. 'Roz will have it in hand. We can only do the best we can for Lizzie and pray it's enough.'

Lizzie was rushed into Resus on their arrival at the hospital.

'Go, team!' Luke began stripping off on his way to the basin. 'We've got to get her as stable as possible before we operate. Dr Gallagher!' he spoke sharply over his shoulder to the other resident who'd been seconded. 'Put another line in the patient's right arm and cannulas in both feet in case we need them. The blood situation could be critical.'

With quick precision Tessa cut through Lizzie's jockey silks. 'IDC in now, please, Roz.'

Roz, who was scrubbed and waiting, deftly inserted the in-dwelling catheter in record time. 'Well done,' Tessa said crisply. 'Now, let's get a theatre gown on her, please. And, Gwyneth, be ready with the space blanket. She's very cold.'

'Right, let's go!' Luke was jamming on a theatre cap as he spoke. 'And bring the life pack, please. We may need to zap her on the way.'

Tessa didn't know what to do.

When her shift ended, Lizzie Collins was still in surgery. Roz had managed to contact the parents and an older brother and they were huddled together, waiting for news. Sue and Iain had gone out for the day and couldn't be contacted. Under the circumstances, Tessa didn't know whether that was a good thing or not.

'Tess, you shouldn't hang about.' There was concern in Drew's eyes. They'd handed over nearly an hour ago. 'From all accounts you've had a hell of a day.'

'I've had better.' Tessa gave a cracked smile. 'I'm just worried Sue might turn up and I'd like to be here for her.'

'We're *all* here for her,' Drew pointed out gruffly. He frowned. 'You can't be all things to everyone, Tess. Especially in this job.'

But I need to see Luke! She could almost hear her strangled voice trying to get out. She swallowed thickly. 'The latest from Theatre is that it's touch and go. There's bruising to Lizzie's internal organs as well.'

'But she's still with us, isn't she?' Drew pointed out calmly. 'And Luke's an outstanding surgeon. If anyone can save her, he can. Go home, Tess,' the charge insisted quietly.

'OK.' Tessa gave in with a little shrug. 'But if you hear anything...'

'I'll phone you,' Drew promised. 'Now, scoot, Sister O'Malley,' he said firmly. 'We need you back here all bright-eyed and bushy-tailed in the morning.'

'Yeah, right.' Tessa made a face but she went anyway.

She went home, showered and changed into cargo pants and a T-shirt. She felt as flat as a burst balloon, all her energy dissipated. Alison was on a late shift so there was no one to talk to—nor confide in—had she been tempted.

It was seven o'clock before Drew got back to her.

'Lizzie's still holding her own.' Drew sounded slightly guarded. 'She took some sorting apparently. Her spleen was ruptured and there was a tear in the bowel. She's in ICU now and stable. If there are no complications tonight, Luke thinks they'll airlift her to Royal Brisbane tomorrow.'

Tessa's knuckled gripped the phone whitely. 'And Luke—is he OK?'

'Actually, he looked done in. I've just had a coffee with him. I think he needed to talk.'

Then why didn't he come to me? Tessa agonised, her knuckles tightening even further on the receiver. Clearly the idea held no attraction for him at all. Her heart was shattering. 'Have they found Sue?' Tessa heard her voice thin and clogged.

'Uh, yes. She arrived about four—just after you left, actually. She's pretty together, propping up the rest of the family.'

'That seems to be the lot of the nurse in the family, doesn't it?' Tessa blinked rapidly. 'I hope it doesn't take too much out of her.'

'I'll keep an eye on her when I can. Tess, I have to go.'

'Thanks for letting me know, Drew.' Tessa put the phone down and stared blindly at the receiver. 'Damn you, Luke Stretton,' she sniffed, palming the sudden wetness away from her eyes. Dropping back on the sofa, she squeezed her eyes shut.

And suddenly, painfully, it became abundantly clear to her. She had never meant as much to Luke as he had to her.

And he wasn't about to come to her, now or ever.

CHAPTER ELEVEN

NEXT morning, Tessa steeled herself to meet Luke on the ward, but he wasn't there. When he hadn't shown up by midmorning, she asked around.

'I heard he was snatching a few days off,' Roz said lightly. 'Gone to Brisbane. By the way.' Roz grinned. 'Our Bradley's pretty chuffed this morning. Did you notice?'

Tessa's mouth lifted briefly at the corners. 'I always knew he'd come good.'

'He's positively blossomed under Luke's leadership.' Roz looked thoughtful. 'I wonder who we'll get to replace him?'

'Brad?'

Roz rolled her eyes. 'Luke, ducky! We've got him for only a few more weeks. We probably should do something about a farewell do. What do you think? You're pretty friendly with him, aren't you?'

Not any longer. Tessa tried to think on her feet. 'Oh, I'm sure whatever you decide will be fine.' She turned quickly back to her paperwork.

For the rest of the day, whenever she thought about Luke Tessa told herself she'd just have to accept that it was never meant to be. Yet she was fully aware that the sense of loss she felt was acute. It would be a long time before she'd trust a man again. Or perhaps she was just a rotten judge of character.

Whatever it was, she was tired of hanging about

like yesterday's newspaper. She had leave owing to her. She'd make her own plans…

That night, she said to Alison over dinner, 'I've applied for a week's leave.'

Alison raised a finely etched brow. 'Are you and Luke…?'

'No!' Tessa shook her head. 'That's over. It wouldn't have worked anyway. He's off to the States soon…'

'What happened?' Alison rested her chin on her hand. 'Lately you've both looked as miserable as sin, if I may say so.'

To her horror, Tessa's vision became blurred. 'It didn't work out, that's all.'

'Perhaps you're misreading things,' Alison sensed her friend's abject misery. 'Why don't you sit him down and talk to him?'

'We've talked. After a fashion,' she qualified bleakly. 'He's totally focused on his career.' Tessa gave a cracked laugh. 'It seems he can't wait to get out of Cressbrook.'

'How long will he be away?'

Tessa swallowed the lump in her throat. 'About a year—'

'That's nothing!' Alison snorted. 'Women managed to wait through years of wars for their men to come back.'

'It's hardly the same, Allie. Anyway, Luke's not my man. He's just someone I met along the way.'

'If you say so.' Alison looked unconvinced. 'So, when are you taking this leave?'

'From tomorrow. And before you ask, I'm going

to throw a few clothes in a bag, get in the Jeep and just drive.'

Tessa headed south to Sydney, deciding that the further away she could get from Luke Stretton the better.

After the first culture shock, she began to enjoy the vibrant busyness of the huge city. Soon she hit her stride, keeping pace with the hurrying masses.

But despite her best efforts, her thoughts would push past the block she'd striven to make emotion-proof, the heady feeling of completeness she'd felt with Luke ambushing her out of nowhere. Oh, he'd probably loved her in his way, but obviously not enough to make any kind of commitment. And that, she reflected, was the sad crux of it.

The house was ablaze with lights when Tessa arrived home on the following Saturday evening. Armed with her suitcase and a couple of carrier bags with designer logos, she struggled up the front steps and into the hallway. Alison came out to greet her.

'Are we having a party?' Tessa laughed as the two friends hugged briefly.

Alison made a face. 'You know how I am, Tess. I hate being home on my own at night. The more lights, the better, as far as I'm concerned. Coffee?'

'Mmm. I'm parched. What's new?' Tessa asked, as they went through to the kitchen.

'Ah.' Alison filled the coffee-maker. 'Quite a bit, actually. I'll fill you in over coffee.'

Cradling her second cup of coffee, Tessa tucked herself into the corner of the lounge. 'Well?' She looked expectantly across at her friend. 'What's this news you've been avoiding telling me for the past half-hour? You're not leaving, are you?'

'Of course not.' Alison looked a bit uncomfortable. 'But Luke has.'

'Left?' Tessa frowned. 'Left work?'

'Left the country,' Alison said carefully. 'Apparently, his place in the training programme came up sooner than expected. He had only a few days to get organised before he flew out.'

Tessa felt an odd sense of unreality. 'So…he's in the States already.'

Alison nodded. 'He phoned last night. He wants you to return his call. He gave me the number, which I've left beside the phone, and the best time to catch him. He said he'll wait around for your call.'

'So now he's thousands of miles away, he's decided it's safe enough to communicate with me!' Tessa said harshly. 'Well, he'll have a long wait!' She wouldn't give him the chance to hurt her again. Not ever.

Six months later, on a Saturday just after eleven, Tessa came off a late shift. Her thoughts were miles away as she stepped out into the car park.

Halfway across to her Jeep, she faltered. Someone, a male figure, was getting out of a car on the other side of the car park. Tessa stopped, her lungs fighting for air. Was it Luke? Surely it was him! Even as she hesitated, his hand came up to flick back his hair from his forehead and she knew for sure.

A whimper of disbelief escaped from her mouth. Panic circled her heart and she thought, If he's come back, it can only mean one thing. She stopped short because her knees had begun to shake dreadfully, and waited for him to come to her.

'It's me, Tess,' he said quietly, and looked straight into her eyes.

She brought her chin up. 'Why are you always frightening the daylights out of me in the dark?'

As a welcome, it didn't have a lot going for it, Luke decided ruefully. Yet in a way he couldn't have explained, her sassy little reprimand was exactly what he needed to hear.

He grinned. 'Haven't lost your quirky sense of humour, I see.'

'Luke?' Tessa's voice shook. 'Tell me I'm not dreaming.'

'I'm right here, Tess. Feel me.' He held out his arms and in a second she was flying into them, being cradled against the solidness of his chest.

'Tess…' He tilted her head up, his voice a murmur against her lips until his mouth caught her own breathy sigh, swallowing it, savouring it, until he claimed her fully with a passion that shook them both to the core.

'Oh!' Tessa exhaled a ragged little breath, running her fingers over his cheekbones, his mouth, the tiny cleft in his chin. 'Is it really you? And what are you doing here?' She buried her face in his chest, breathing in the warm male closeness of him like life-giving oxygen.

After a moment he said, 'If we can get out of this damned car park, I'll tell you.'

For answer, she snuggled closer. 'I thought I saw you get out of a car.'

'Mmm. A hire car. I've come straight from Brisbane airport.'

'Heavens! How long have you been travelling?'

'Too long.' He released her then slid his hand down her arm to mesh her fingers with his. 'Do you think you could take me home?'

'Alison's away on days off,' Tessa said a little later, turning back to him almost shyly as she unlocked the front door and went ahead of him into the hall.

Luke's mouth twitched. 'So we have the place to ourselves.'

'Do you have a bag or something?' Tessa brushed a curl behind her ear.

'In the boot. I'll get it later.'

'Oh, OK. Are you hungry?'

He shook his head. 'I wouldn't mind a shower, though.'

'Me, too.' She blushed. 'I mean, I need to get out of this grubby uniform and—'

'Tessa,' he said gently, touching a hand to her hair, lingering over its rich mahogany silkiness, '*We'll* have a shower.'

He pulled her into the bathroom and set about undressing them both. Turning on the shower, Luke waited until the water ran warm then he reached out and tugged her to stand with him beneath the jets. He gently began to soap her—and it began all over again. That mindless, loving feeling, that boneless melting, that coming together as though they'd never been apart…

Gazing at him, the slight flush along his cheekbones, Tessa decided that his eyes had never seemed so blue. 'This is crazy.' She hid her emotion in humour, stifling a giggle against his chest.

'Speak for yourself,' Luke sounded offended. 'There's nothing crazy about me.' Reaching behind him, he closed off the taps. 'I love you, Tess.' Turning her face up to his, he stared down into her wide eyes. 'Marry me,' he said throatily. 'I don't want to spend another day without you.'

'Oh, Luke.'

His eyes held hers. 'Say, yes—please.'

His blue eyes were steady, waiting. She could hardly breathe. But she did manage to whisper, 'Yes, please, Luke. I want to marry you more than anything in the world—and I, too, love you. Oh.' She giggled and put a finger against her lips. 'That sounded like a song.'

Luke grinned. 'Sing away. I kept wanting to yodel when I got off the plane. Do you think we need counselling?'

'Idiot…' Tessa tilted her back and smiled tenderly. 'Take me to bed.'

They woke very early.

'How much leave do you have?' Tessa asked, adrift in something that was so delicious she wanted to stay floating there for ever.

Luke kissed her softly on her cheek, her chin, her throat. 'Just under two weeks.'

'Then we shouldn't waste a minute of it. Come on.' She tugged him. 'Get up, we've plans to make.'

Luke groaned. 'I'm jet-lagged, Tess.'

'You can be jet-lagged tomorrow.' She flew out of bed. 'I feel like tea and lashings of toast.'

They planned their wedding a week on Saturday. 'Your mum thought a garden wedding.' Luke took another slice of toast.

'You've talked to my mother?'

'And your father. I asked him for your hand.'

Tessa snickered. 'That's a bit old-fashioned.'

'I'm an old-fashioned guy.' His face worked for a moment. 'I never meant to leave the way I did, Tess. But you'd gone on holidays and suddenly there was just no time left to try to sort anything out between us.'

'No.' Tessa looked down into her teamug. 'I couldn't bring myself to phone you either. And I'm sorry about that.' She gnawed on her bottom lip. 'I thought you'd given up on us.'

'I'm sorry it seemed like that,' he said quietly. 'But back then I felt I had nothing to offer you.'

Tessa looked at him earnestly. 'Your money, or lack of it, was never a consideration for me. I loved Luke Stretton, the man. The rest would have been only window-dressing.'

He rubbed a hand across his face. 'I see a lot of things more clearly now. You're the most precious thing in the world to me, Tess.'

For once in her life, Tessa couldn't speak. Instead, she reached out and placed her palm against his cheek. After a while, she asked dreamily, 'Will I like living in Louisville?'

'You will. I have an apartment. It's nice but it needs your touch to make it home. And, of course, we're in the state of Kentucky. Lots of top-notch horse studs for you to visit.'

'I'll enjoy that…' Tessa felt a funny lump in her

throat. 'Will you work in Brisbane when we come back, do you think?'

There was a gleam in his blue eyes. 'The Prince Charles Hospital has already shown some interest. Will you mind living in the city again?'

'Of course not,' she chided gently. 'I've always thought a wife's place is with her husband. And we can still use Half Moon for weekends and holidays, can't we?'

'Sounds perfect.' A slow smile curved his lips. 'Speaking of Half Moon, how is Del these days?'

Tessa laughed, a bit off-key. 'Enjoying life in Brisbane. Mum and Dad have built her a little flat at their place. She's discovered the internet and genealogy, which is keeping her very busy.'

'I thought you said she hadn't settled.'

She flushed faintly. 'I might have fibbed there. They were rather desperate times, if you recall.'

'Yes.' Luke's mouth tightened. 'I'm sorry, Tess.'

'You don't need to keep apologising,' she cajoled softly. 'We both made stupid mistakes. But we're back on track now—aren't we?'

'You'd better believe it.' And then his arms were around her and he settled her on his lap, drawing her close to the clamour of his heart. And Tessa clung to him, knowing they'd at last forgiven each other for all the hurt.

Luke rested his chin on her hair. 'So, now we're all squared away, fill me in on the local gossip. Has Sue had her baby?'

'Yes.' Tessa tucked herself more closely against him. 'A little boy, Toby. He's gorgeous. And

Gwyneth left soon after you did. She joined one of the airlines as cabin crew.'

Luke bit back a wry grin. 'I don't think her heart was ever in hospital nursing. Did she go for the airline's snappy uniform by any chance?'

Tessa huffed. 'She did mention it in passing. Oh, and John Abbott went back to his family in Melbourne. He came in one day to say goodbye and to thank us—well, you, really.'

'How did he seem?' Luke's eyes lit up with satisfaction.

Tessa lifted a shoulder. 'Clean and tidy, very together.' She looked thoughtful for a moment. 'He has you to thank for giving him back his life.'

'That's my job, Tess,' he dismissed gruffly. 'It's what I trained for.'

Tessa blocked a yawn. 'This was a mad idea, getting up so early. Let's go back to bed for a while. We'll make the rest of our plans a bit later—if that's OK with you?'

'Absolutely.' Luke smiled indulgently, brushing his fingers down the side of her face. 'I love you, my green-eyed girl. You're my life and my love.'

'And you're mine, Luke Stretton. For ever.' Tessa thought her heart would burst. She put a hand up to touch his face, seeing his eyes reflecting what was surely in his heart. And in hers.

What she'd thought they'd lost had been found, only now it was so much more. Now the road ahead was all sparkling, new, untouched. The road they would travel together.